OUT OF THE GATE

A GOLD RUSH RANCH ORIGIN STORY

ELSIE SILVER

Cover by Wildheart Designs

Editing by Rochelle J. Simas at IDK Art

❀ Created with Vellum

For all the girls whose best use for flowers was braiding them into their horse's mane.

"Why are you so sad?

"Because you speak to me in words and I look at you with feelings."

LEO TOLSTOY

CONTENTS

1

ADA

I HIT the hard dirt with a loud thud that echoes through my bones. My teeth rattle at the impact and I feel a small rock pressing into my right shoulder blade. I close my eyes and groan at the sound of galloping hooves rumbling across the ground.

Again. She tossed me again.

I'm a farm girl, we're raised hardy. But good lord—my eyes flutter shut—this filly is going to be the death of me. All I want to do is spend my summer break away from university, training my new project horse. I want to be the one to sit on her for the first time, maybe walk around in a small circle. My expectations are pretty low. But she is not having it.

Footsteps approach and I still don't open my eyes. I know all the ranch hands think my project is a great joke and, frankly, I don't want to hear about it.

I'm probably fine. Bruised to hell and sore tomorrow, but fine. Right now, if I don't move, nothing hurts. So maybe I'll just stay here? Live out my life laying in the field.

A noisy sigh rushes past my lips as I take an inventory of my aching body.

Toes and fingers still wiggle.

Head still turns side to side.

"You alive, Goldilocks?"

Heart stops beating.

Eyes squeeze shut even harder.

That voice. I'm pretty sure my blood stops pumping and pools in my beet red cheeks.

"Coulda sworn I taught you better than that."

My lungs empty painfully, all the air rushing out in a gasp.

Dermot Harding.

My heart slams back into action, rioting behind my ribs as I lift my hands to scrub my face. Not wanting to even look at him, because I know what I'll see. The single most attractive man I've ever known; older and out of my league. The man I've spent the last three years trying to get over. The childhood crush that I've never outgrown.

The man I've loved since I was a ten-year-old girl.

When I finally decide to pry my eyes open, he's looking down over me, blocking out the direct sun but wearing its rays like a halo. Smirking.

My body melts into a pathetic, speechless puddle of a love-struck girl right at his feet. I forget about my horse. I forget where I am. I just stare at him, thinking that I could probably just lay here under his glow and be happy.

And then the anger hits. *Three long years.* Not a letter. No word. *Nothing.* I latch on to that feeling, knowing I'll need it to maintain my strength. That inner fire and fury will be the only thing that keeps me from falling down the same rabbit hole as before. I haven't worked this hard at moving on to end up there again.

"You're back." *Obviously, Ada. You idiot.* I blink my eyes like I can't quite believe he's here. Standing over me, in the flesh, after so long. "When did you get back?"

He reaches one broad palm out to help me up. "A couple months ago."

I place my hand in his and struggle to swallow a small whimper when we make contact. Instead, I just make an awkward gurgling noise. I swear my entire body comes alive when he's around, it's like an electric current shoots up my arm. Touching him is akin to resting my finger on one of the live fences around here—it always has been. For me anyway.

His eyes widen imperceptibly as he pulls me to standing and then he yanks his hand back, as though I'm diseased or something. Like he can't stand touching me. Like *that* night all over again.

Clearing my throat, I dust my jeans off and roll my shoulders back, then jut my chin up proudly. I refuse to crumble around him. I have nothing to be embarrassed about. I'm an adult now, a university student—I've lived my life. Had boyfriends. Grown up. *Moved on.*

We all make regrettable choices when we're lovesick teenagers.

From the corner of my eye, I see my filly, Penny,

grazing happily by the fence. Not feeling the least bit bad about bucking me off. Apparently, she's glad to be rid of me and *that's* the exact energy I need to channel too.

He's been home for months and hasn't thought to come see us? Feelings of inadequacy sour my voice when I finally respond with, "And you're just stopping by now?"

Dermot shoves his hands in his pockets and kicks at the ground. "I needed some time to get right after my tour. To unwind."

The gravel in his tone has my eyes snapping up to scour his form before me. Here I am acting like a petulant child, not even considering how his time in the army may have impacted him.

I drink him in like a cold soda on a hot day. Annoyingly, he's just as delicious as I remember. With a dropping sensation in my gut, I'm forced to admit he might be even more stunning than ever. He looks more densely muscled, broader, more mature—he must be thirty-one now. Dark shadows move behind his fathomless eyes, like a man who's seen too much.

But that doesn't matter, he's more painfully irresistible than ever before. Hawkish dark brown eyes and even darker hair, strong masculine features that still somehow manage not to look too coarse. The perfect dusting of scruff over shapely lips.

Lips that hadn't moved at all beneath mine that night.

Big hands that could circle my entire waist. Dermot is tall and imposing, a farm boy through and through, and I feel like a delicate little bird next to him. A bird that has been chirping around his head, seeking attention for years.

A bird that he batted away three years ago before leaving the ranch—the country.

I'd stood on his balcony, eyes shrink-wrapped in tears at the knowledge he'd be leaving, and a voice thick with longing. I'd told him I'd miss him, I told him I loved him. And then I'd stood up on my tippy toes, slid my hands over his muscular shoulders and pressed my lips against his while he stood there completely frozen. "Ada, you can't do this, you're too young," he'd said with pity in his eyes as he gently pushed me away.

The memory still makes me cringe. Makes my throat feel hot and dry. It could still make me cry, if I let it. But I finished crying over Dermot Harding a long time ago. I've moved on.

"Why are you here?" My voice sounds wobbly even to my own ears, and I cross my arms to hide my shaking hands.

"Your dad asked me to come down and break some youngsters for him." He grins at me, melting my panties. *You're still pathetic, Ada.* "He says no one starts a horse better than I do."

I scoff with forced amusement, meeting the warmth of his eyes. A soft, alluring brown, like the saddles I spent hours oiling on a fence while watching him break the young horses every summer. The perfect contrast against the bright green valley of Ruby Creek that leads out to the steep North Cascades mountain range.

"And after watching you just now, I have to say... I

might know why he thinks that." He winks, always cocky and joking. Like nothing monumental ever happened between us.

"Yeah, yeah." I shake my head as I turn to walk towards Penny. "It's great to see you too, Dermot," I add from over my shoulder, not able to look at him any longer.

"You want help with the filly?" I stop mid-step, surprised by the offer.

"Do you have time?" I call back, trying to act casual as I continue my approach towards the beautiful copper-colored filly.

"Spending a few weeks, so yup."

My breathing goes shallow. *A few weeks?* I'm going to have to deal with my haywire hormones, years old embarrassment, and fluttering stomach for *a few weeks?* "Okay, great!" It comes out a little too brightly, making me wince. "You're a twenty-one-year-old woman, Ada, get your shit together," I mutter to myself as I grab a hold of Penny's bridle and turn back towards where Dermot is still standing, looking at me quizzically.

"Tomorrow afternoon? I'll work the others in the morning," he nods towards Penny, "then you can tell me all about Big Red here."

I just give him an awkward thumbs up and turn back towards the barn, feeling his eyes roam my retreating figure like a spray of warm water across my back.

Time alone with Dermot Harding? Lord, help me.

———

"YOUR VERY OWN RACEHORSE, HUH?" Dermot drawls, the river babbling quietly behind him.

I trail my fingers over Penny's silky forehead, nodding and admiring her intelligent eyes—maybe a little too intelligent for my own good. I know deep down it will all be worth it when I can convince her to give me a shot. My daddy didn't raise his only child to be a quitter. But hitting the dirt day in and out is demotivating, not to mention painful.

Dermot chuckles. "Can't fault you for knowing what you want. You've been on about wanting to get into race-horses since you were a little kid. Picked yourself a hell of a challenge to start with."

"That's what everyone keeps telling me," I say, unable to tear my eyes away from where he's tightening the cinch on my saddle. The way his tanned forearms ripple and flex as he ties the leather off there is like dirty talk for the most primal parts of my brain. My tongue darts out, wetting my bottom lip as he pats the filly's neck and I let my eyes trail the veins that run down the top of his firm hand.

For crying out loud, Ada. You're lusting after a man's veins.

I promised myself I was going to play it cool today. But I'd obviously lied, because I wasn't playing it cool right now, or first thing when I woke up this morning and imagined him moving over top of me, inside of me. Our movements jerky, hard, and fevered in my mind's eye.

Yeah, I'd imagined hate sex with Dermot Harding for the first time in a long time and now I'm a nervous wreck around him. Knowing he's sleeping across the driveway in the little laneway house after all this time apart? It's almost too much.

We left so much unsaid between us, and now everything feels awkward and strained. For me, anyway. He seems completely unaffected. Like the same easy-going, unflappable Dermot I've always known. But that's probably how most responsible adults react to an eighteen-year-old girl kissing them. For him it was probably a funny, teenaged blip in the radar. The bubbling over of wild hormones for a young girl stuck on a ranch for too long.

But for me it was the memory that still had the power to make me blush, the hot lance of disappointment that kept me up at night to this day. One of my greatest mistakes.

His hand lands on my shoulder, and I startle. "You ready? I'm going to hop on Solar and then pony Penny into the water. Once I get her knee deep in the river, you can get on. In the water she won't be able to turn into a bucking bronco, and hopefully having an experienced horse beside her will help her stay calm."

The heat from his body seeps into mine, making me almost too hot under the high summer sun. I give him a terse nod, steeling myself. We lead Penny and my dad's favorite ranch horse, Solar, down to the river behind the small guesthouse where Dermot lives when he stays on the ranch. His family farm in Merritt is just far enough away that staying on site makes the most sense.

I take a deep breath, determination clear on my face

as I approach my thoroughbred filly. Dermot swings one powerful leg over Solar's broad back with Penny's rope tight in his hand and coaxes her into the gentle current. Once they're deep enough, I walk in, feeling the cold bite of the mountain water against my ankles. "Hey, little girl," I rub my hand along her flank reassuringly, "how about we try this again, huh? I'll be good to you if you're good to me."

Dermot snorts and my eyes narrow. "Something funny?"

"Yeah. You're going to spoil this horse even if she's not good to you."

Does he even realize what he just so casually implied? I shake my head and turn away, chest searing with the sharp lance of indignation. "I guess you'd know," I bite out as I lift my boot into the stirrup at her side.

"Ada..." He trails off, but I ignore him and step up, leaning against Penny's back. I feel her go rigid beneath my weight, anticipating my leg swinging up through her peripheral vision.

"Easy, girl," Dermot coos now, his voice all deep and soothing as I run my hand up her neck, just waiting a few moments to let her hopefully relax a bit. When I hear her loud snort, I decide to take my chances and ever so slowly lift my leg over the saddle.

I squeeze my core, trying to sit down as gently as possible. Letting my body hover before I come to rest on her back, softly. I feel her start ever so slightly and then go still.

I lift my head slowly, not wanting to break the

tenuous agreement we seem to have come to, and look up at Dermot as a wide genuine smile takes over my face. It's been at least ten seconds and I'm still sitting on her. Her ears are flicking back and forth uncertainly, and her body is tense—but I'm still here!

Dermot's perfectly white teeth glint back at me as he gives me a proud shake of his head.

And then, with a squeal, Penny rears straight up. Her neck fills the space in front of me as she stands on her back legs. Her reflexes so quick that I don't even feel it coming.

Before I can even grab mane, I'm unceremoniously dumped into the freezing river water.

2

DERMOT

"ADA!" At first, I want to laugh. Her face went from shit-eating-grin to unadulterated shock so damn fast. But then she toppled backwards into the water. And now all I can feel is pure panic coursing through my veins. She has to be okay.

I tie the filly's rope around the horn of the saddle and jump off my horse, the sound of her scream still lingering in my ears. My steps feel heavy and awkward as I trudge through the river towards the other side where she fell.

"Fuck!" Her open palm lands on the water with a loud slap, and I see the horses startle behind me.

Ada is kneeling on the riverbed, chest deep in the water that's surrounding her petite form. She's soaked from head to toe, her golden hair dark with wetness and slicked down against the elegant curve of her neck.

"Are you okay?" I keep moving towards her. I have to make sure she's alright. Much like yesterday, I can't force myself away from her—even though I should. I can't stop scanning her doll-like face, comparing it to all the nights I laid on my cot and tried to recall the way she looks. Imagining Ada's face, every curve, every freckle, was like therapy—a distraction from the much more violent images running through my mind every night.

Ada's fresh face, replaying that kiss; it all became my only lifeline to the real world during a time when I was knee-deep in blood, gore, and depression.

"I don't think I've ever heard you swear before," I say, falling onto my knees in front of her and resting my hands on her shoulders.

She scrubs her hands across her face and back over her head. "That's because you haven't known me since I was eighteen! And yeah, I'm *fucking* sick of falling off."

Okay. So, she's mad. Even someone as emotionally numb as I am can figure that much out. "Does it hurt anywhere?" My eyes dart all over her body, looking for signs of distress. My hands flutter down over her toned arms, feeling for possible broken bones. *Mr. Wilson will kill me if she's injured.*

"I'm fine." She sighs. "I mean, I hurt everywhere. That's what falling off every damn day gets you."

I grip her by the ribs, I can feel the thick strap of her bra through her thin wet shirt as I pull her towards me and stand us both up. She comes to stand easily and everything seems to be in working order. I rake my gaze up over her curves, prepared to make a smart remark about how if she doesn't want to be sore she should stop falling off, but I stop when I get to her soaked tank top.

The one plastered onto her body, leaving absolutely

nothing to the imagination. The taper of her waist, the swell of her breasts, the hard points of her nipples so clear through the wet fabric.

My throat goes dry and I groan, squeezing my eyes shut and looking away. Nothing good can come from admiring Ada like this. That kiss three years ago woke a sleeping giant inside my mind, opened my eyes to possibilities I'd *never* considered. Ada had always been just another farm kid to me—until she wasn't.

I've been almost constantly reminding myself that she's still the young daughter of a man I've known and respected for years; a man who has become my friend, almost family. She's still the girl all of Ruby Creek knows and loves. A girl that same town would whisper about if something were to happen with the older ranch hand who's been hanging around since she was a child. There is absolutely no way around how inappropriate that would seem, and I refuse to torpedo her reputation like that. I've had three years to mull over the options, and the only feasible one is that I need to stay the fuck away from her.

Plus, a woman like Ada deserves better than me. So I tear my eyes up and away from her body, only to be met with the equally tempting heart shape of her slightly parted lips, the spray of soft freckles across her bronzed cheeks, and those wide emerald green eyes.

The green eyes in which I watched a heart break three years ago. The green eyes that have haunted my dreams every night since. The green eyes that have looked at me like I hung the moon for years.

And now? A look full of longing and promise that a man like me shouldn't get used to.

Ada Wilson out of bounds.

I trail my hands down over her hips, relishing the feel of her body in my grasp. Wanting to pull her closer. I settle with inclining my head in towards her, seeking that signature scent that I've spent three years trying to commit to memory. My fingers pulse, squeezing her waist, and my words come out rough. "Are you sure you're okay?"

"Yes." Her voice is soft and slightly breathless. A raspy whisper that feels like silk on my skin.

She stares up at me with a fire that wasn't there before, like she can't decide between mauling me or drowning me. Her eyes twinkle as she drinks me in. And I let her—because fuck, does it ever feel good to have a woman like Ada Wilson look at you like *this*. Her hand comes up, and she trails her dainty fingers delicately over my cheekbone like she might break me or spook me. *Like last time.*

"Dermot... I—" Her voice cracks a little, and damn if I don't feel a guilty pinch in my chest at her show of emotion. I should put a stop to this, I really should.

"Ada. You shouldn't look at me like this."

She presses a finger to my lips to silence me and quirks one shapely brow up in challenge as she bites back, "Why would you care how I look at you?" The pads of her fingers brush up over the bridge of my nose and then across the peak of my brow, as though she's reading braille. Like my features might tell her a story, give her some answers. She drags her nails across my scalp, sending a spray of goosebumps down the back of my tense arms, "You've made it very clear how you feel about me." Her hands fall away and she looks me straight in the eye as she delivers her killing blow. "And anyway, I've moved on."

Then Ada pushes off of me as she moves past my immobilized form. I feel the heavy thump of my heart against my sternum. *Made my feelings clear?* Of course that's what she thinks. I've never told her otherwise. Nor will I.

In the months since I got home, I've tried to prepare myself for eventually seeing Ada again. I've worked hard at talking myself into believing that the chemistry I keep recalling from that night was all in my head. A shocking memory riddled by my intense longing to be back somewhere safe, away from the sounds of whizzing bullets and pained screams. My plan was to be cool, calm, slightly removed. But then I laid eyes on her, laid out flat on the grass like a flower in the sun just begging to be picked, and my resolve started to crumble.

Now I'm constantly reminding myself that she's the ranch owner's daughter, and that I'm just the ranch hand who comes by to break his young horses every summer. *That's it. That's all.*

"Let's go," I grumble, and it comes out more harshly than I intend. But a rough tone is going to hurt her a lot less in the long run than thinking a man like me will ever be able to give her what she needs. What she deserves.

She unwraps her filly's reins and takes off up the river bank, her stride stiff and her head held high.

"You can't be doing this, Dermot." I mutter as I grab Solar's reins and follow in her footsteps, lost in thought. It's safe to assume she's not listening by how far ahead she is. At the very least, she doesn't look back. Which is a good thing, because I know I've got desire written all over my face.

I shake my head and kick a rock as I forge ahead. I'm too old, too set in my ways, and after the things I saw on tour, I've retreated too far into myself to ever truly share my life with someone—especially someone as vivacious as Ada. She deserves to see and do it all, not be stifled by someone who hits the ground when he hears a loud noise.

I need to stay away from her. For her, and for myself. I've got a habit of sending people running. My parents could hardly wait for me to turn eighteen before they packed up and moved somewhere warm. They never visit and barely call. Girlfriends never last. And even friends I made in the army have either fallen out of touch or just plain never made it back. Everyone leaves, and Ada would eventually too.

Gold Rush Ranch is a slice of heaven. The Wilson's vast swath of land here in Ruby Creek sits in a picturesque little valley where tourists visit to seek a hairy mythical creature on Sasquatch Mountain. It's bright and sunny here, just like Ada.

My farm up in Merritt is cold and stark, the mountain peaks are so high that I feel almost claustrophobic sometimes, especially when the place gets snowed in. It's what my parents left me after they retired and moved south. None of my siblings wanted it. Apparently I'm a sentimental sap, because even though I'm not actually doing anything with the land, the thought of handing it over to someone else is more than I can bear.

And it's definitely not the place for Ada.

Which is fine, because I'm definitely not the man for her either. No matter how she looks at me or how my cock twitches against my jeans when she touches me.

After storming to the barn, we untack wordlessly beside each other. I sneak looks at Ada as she moves around the filly, brushing her a little more vigorously than necessary. It almost makes me chuckle. Leave it to Ada to want a racehorse when her dad has fields full of top end ranch horses. She always was one to want something she shouldn't.

I pull the saddle off of Solar and manage to bite out, "Same time and place tomorrow. I'll get on her though."

She bristles and rolls her shoulders back. "Take a hike, Dermot. She's my horse. I'm breaking her. Help, don't help, I don't care. But you sure as hell will not waltz in here and take over *my* project." Her hand flails up above her head. "I've had it up to here with people telling me what I can and can't do." She spins on her heel then, and storms off with the fiery little filly prancing along beside her.

As I watch her leave, I realize that Ada Wilson is not the same girl I left on that porch three years ago.

———

"OKAY, GIVE ME A LEG UP," Ada says, turning her ass towards me. I take a deep swallow, feeling my Adam's apple bob in my throat. Giving someone a leg up onto their horse isn't special, but it doesn't fall squarely into my *Don't Touch Ada Wilson* plan either.

I step up behind her, breathing in the scent of her tangerine lotion. It suits her, bright and citrusy—intoxicating. She lifts one leg and waits for me to help her. Bending down, I wrap my palm around her slender calf, willing myself not to trail my hand up further.

She looks back over her shoulder at me, probably wondering what the holdup is, and for a moment our eyes lock. I take a deep dive into the emerald depths of her irises. So wide and expressive, and for once since I got back they don't look angry. I hold them with my gaze, just enjoying looking at her.

Bad idea.

I shake my head and clear my throat. "One. Two. Three." On three I toss her up, but am slow to let go of her leg. I can't seem to tear my eyes away from the way my hand looks on her. The contrast, the compliment. Soft and hard. Sunny and dark. Young and old. *Older.* I refuse to consider myself old at thirty-one.

Either way, nothing about us matches. Ada and I are a dichotomy, opposites, like two ends of a magnet that can't seem to stay away from each other no matter how fucked up it is.

"Dermot?" She asks, her expression quizzical. "You okay?"

I yank my hands off her leg and step back abruptly,

offering an, "All good," over my shoulder as I duck out of the round pen and turn to lean on it as casually as I can manage.

Ada ignores the awkward moment and gets to riding. She looks so damn pleased with herself as she trots around on her leggy filly and pride swells in my chest. This girl is tough as nails, not a quitter's bone in her body. We've spent the rest of the week working on Penny—a chestnut mare through and through. She pulls out an awful lot of acrobatics, but Ada sticks on every time and after one week she's got her walking and trotting in the round pen unassisted. Not half bad.

Where the filly has flourished, interactions between Ada and I are strained. She can barely look at me since that day in the river and I'm so busy trying not to stare at her body, the way her hips sway in the saddle, that I feel like all I do is make things more awkward by staring at her face instead.

The way her tongue darts out to wet her lower lip, the ways she purses her mouth when she's concentrating, the small genuine smiles she gives Penny that make the corners of her eyes crinkle.

Everything about her is downright distracting. Maybe I'm better off only looking at her ponytail? I stare at it, watching it sway. I could wrap it around my hand, give it a good hard tug, and...

My forehead falls onto the top fence panel in defeat. *I am fucked.*

I've known Ada since she was a buck-toothed, knobby-kneed ten-year-old. She used to burn around here on her bike, getting messy and getting into trouble. A true ranch rat in every sense of the word. The only child of one of the most hard-working, loving, and respectable couples I've ever known. It didn't surprise me at all when I came back summer after summer and saw her growing into a remarkable young woman.

I would have expected nothing less. But she was still just little Goldilocks to me. I still saw tangled blonde hair and cheeks smudged with purple from feasting on wild blackberries when I looked at her.

Sure, her obvious crush had been a running joke around the ranch when she was little. She'd follow me everywhere, make excuses to do things with me. Chat my ear off about horses, so full of questions. I was a twenty-year-old man, and I was awkward as all get out, especially when the other staff and even Mr. Wilson would rib me about it. It was endearing, really. But eventually everyone stopped talking about it, and I assumed she'd outgrown it. A childhood crush to look back on fondly.

Until she kissed me.

She'd shocked me into stillness when she'd cupped my jaw and pressed her plush, heart-shaped lips against mine. Clearly, with age, she'd just gotten really fucking adept at hiding her feelings.

"Be safe, Dermot. I love you," she'd said. And I'd pushed her back from me like it meant nothing and told her she should go. The look in her eyes that night? The way they'd welled up as she traced her fingers across the bow of her top lip? *Fuck.*

That look haunts me to this day. I can feel it like a weight on my chest.

I'd never wanted to hurt Ada. In fact, I've always known I would kill anyone who did. But that night, she planted a seed of possibility in my mind. And its vines grew fast and reckless, altering my sense of right and wrong, warping my memories, and changing everything I was supposed to feel about Ada Wilson.

That seed has left me battling myself for the last three years. Battling against wishing I'd fisted her hair and kissed her back. Hard. Shown her what a man could do, what a man could make her feel.

But I couldn't. Ada belongs firmly in the *My Friend's Daughter* column and also in the *She's Way Too Fucking Young For You* column.

Which is why, as we're wrapping up on Friday afternoon, I try to make casual conversation after a week's worth of tension between us. "She's looking good, Ada. You should be proud of yourself. Penny's not an easy horse."

She smiles as she strokes the filly's forelock lovingly and muses, "The payoff on something easy never feels as sweet though, does it? I like a challenge."

I clear my throat. I must be obsessed because everything this woman says sounds like a metaphor to me.

"Next week we gallop?"

She turns and grins at me. "Next week we gallop."

And then I'm down on the ground. A loud bang flattening me almost instantly. I drop so quickly that I barely remember getting here. I wrap my arms around the back of my head waiting for another bang to come. Another explosion. More screams. The tch-tch-tch of bullets spraying everywhere. All I know is that I have to protect myself so that I can get home safely.

It's only when I feel a soft hand stroking soothingly between my shoulders and Ada's soft sugary voice saying, "I'm right here. It was just a truck backfiring. You're okay," that I start to realize where I am and what I've done. The flashes like this come hard and fast, there's no predicting them. And there's no avoiding them.

"Dermot?" Her hand moves up to massage the back of my neck as I pant into the dusty earth beneath me, trying to calm the erratic beating of my heart. "What can I do for you?"

"Nothing." I whisper raggedly, still unable to move. "Just give me a couple of minutes."

I expect her to walk away, but instead she ties her filly up and then lays down right on the ground beside me, going back to stroking my back quietly. She doesn't ask me questions, she doesn't rush me, she just stays with me.

After a few minutes the anxiety of the moment passes and I feel my breathing normalize again. I peek over at her, laying facing me with her head propped in her hand, wide green eyes regarding me carefully. She might be acting calm but she looks scared. *This is why you're no good for her.*

"I'm okay."

"Are you sure?" Her brows knit together in concern.

"Yes." I roll onto my back to look up at the sky,

remind myself of where I am. Ada does the same, but reaches between us to wrap her small hand around mine. She squeezes it tightly. Once. Twice. Three times. A simple enough gesture, but one that has a line of electricity buzzing up my forearm into my inner elbow. An ache. A dangerous current flowing between us.

I pull my hand away, resting both of them on my stomach, and try to lighten the mood. "We've got to stop meeting like this."

She chuckles, but it's a little brittle. A little forced. So I look over at her and try again, not wanting to talk about what just happened. "Friday night. Big plans, Goldilocks?"

She presses her lips together. "Actually, yeah. Meeting up at Neighbor's Pub in town."

"Meeting up?" I waggle my eyebrows jokingly. "Like a date?"

She turns her head, eyes like beams straight into mine. Something sad shining in the sage-colored highlights of her irises. "Yes, Dermot. Like a date."

And then she gets up and walks away. Leaving me alone with an entirely different and unfamiliar type of green-eyed monster.

Maybe it's time to catch Ada up on the torture she's put me through for the last three years.

3

ADA

MY DATE SUCKED.

I buckle my seat belt and turn the key in the ignition. Shaking my head as I pull out onto the road that heads home. Ready to berate myself the whole way back.

I spent the entire time thinking about Dermot, wishing it were him I was out with but also wanting to kick him in the balls for ditching and then coming back like nothing happened. And then wanting to wrap him in my arms and fend off all the demons he's been living with. Just thinking about Dermot, strong and proud, cowering on the ground makes my eyes well with emotion—makes my chest ache for him.

I still want him, demons and all. And I hate it.

What's worse, is that day in the river he didn't even deny that he's made his feelings about me clear. He's supposed to feel nothing for me, except maybe some sort of brotherly love. But I'm not a virginal teenager anymore, I didn't miss the way his eyes burned across my skin, the way his firm hands pulsed around my waist as he drank me in. This desperate little part of me had thought he'd maybe change his mind and spill the words about how badly he wants me, like in one of those books my mom hides under her mattress. *Talk about tragic.*

I've been telling myself that I'm over him, that I've moved on. But apparently my heart missed the memo. I've tried. I've had boyfriends at university. But they never last, and they never make my heart pound. They never keep me up at night, thinking about how their hands would feel gliding over my fevered skin. And even when we get to that point, it's fun but... lacking. There's no fire. No passion. No knocking the art of the walls. I want that messy, desperate, gasping for air kind of sex.

Travis, my date from tonight, is a nice enough guy, but we've been friends since before we could talk and we still feel like just friends now. We've been out a few times, but I know it's not going anywhere. Pickings are slim in a small town like Ruby Creek, and as I drive back to the ranch, I find myself wishing I could settle for a guy like Travis Bennett. Wishing I could be interested in cattle ranching. It was the family business, after all.

But instead, I spend my days dreaming about Dermot Harding and thoroughbred racing.

My parents drive us in to Vancouver every summer for the Denman Derby. A full day to watch the races. I look forward to that one special day every year, to the anticipation I feel when the bell rings and the gates flash open. To the rumble of hooves that shake the ground as the horses thunder past. There's just *something* about the whole sport.

I want to be a part of it.

And I want Dermot Harding. Stupidly, obsessively, pathetically—the feelings are seeping out through the seams of the carefully constructed box I tucked them away in. For the past three years, I've easily contained them in the *Never Gonna Happen* section of my brain. But that was before he touched me, before I knew what his calloused palms felt like sliding across my arms. Gripping my waist.

Before he hit me with a look so full of tortured longing that it took my breath away and made me flee. A look that has been living in my head for a week, bouncing around like a pinball machine. Giving me a goddamn headache.

So I went on a stupid date. Thinking I could clear my head, but boy was I wrong. Now all I am is agitated that I wasted my own time and possibly gave a friend false hope for something more. "Great work, Ada," I mutter as I pull into the ranch and park in front of the main farmhouse. Slamming the door harder than I should, I round the back of my car towards the path that leads to the front door.

Which of course takes me right past the small laneway house that my parents built for guests. The one that Dermot stays in when he's here. The one with *the* porch.

"You trying to injure that car, Goldilocks?"

He's sitting on the weathered swing that looks out towards the mountains with a glass of amber liquid in his hand. The mellow glow of the outdoor lights highlight the strong planes of his masculine face, the inky shine of his hair, and the brightness of his fresh white t-shirt. I imagine the shirt wet like in the river earlier this week, remembering the way it clung to the defined lines in his chest and hung suggestively over the deep V that disappeared beneath his waistband.

My mouth goes instantly dry at the memory.

I stop and face him, sick of holding my tongue. *Sick of feeling so lovesick.* "Better than injuring you, wouldn't you say?"

"Ada—"

"No. Don't *Ada* me. I'm not in the mood."

I move to keep walking, wanting to put distance between us before I say something I'll really regret, but he stops me in my tracks when he says, "Okay then. How was your date?"

There's a bite in his words that I don't entirely appreciate, not considering the way he's all but disappeared for the last three years. Now he's going to waltz in and act like he has some sort of claim on me? Nah. He's not entitled to that tone where I'm concerned.

I storm up the two steps towards him, hand gripping the railing so hard that I feel the edges of the wood bite into my fingers almost painfully. "It was great." I lie through my teeth with a confidence that doesn't match my inner turmoil. "Travis is great."

Dermot swaggers across the porch, all confidence and maturity, while I feel like I'm shaking in my boots, holding myself up on the railing like a crutch. So I step up, refusing to back away and give him the win, pressing myself against the vertical beam for support, gripping the railing that carries on around the deck.

Braced and ready for battle.

He comes close, too close, invading my space and stealing all the surrounding oxygen, like he just absorbs it with his presence alone. "Travis..." He rolls the name around in his mouth like he's tasting it, examining the flavor. He's close enough that I feel his breath fan across my collarbones, a small reprieve from the heavy mugginess that pervades the night air.

I watch him swirl his drink casually, ice clinking against the heavy glass. "Does Travis send goosebumps up your arms just by coming close?"

I glance down to confirm what he's talking about. *Dick.* I jut my chin out defiantly. "Travis is good for me."

"Anyone would be better for you than me."

An unladylike snort escapes me. "No shit."

He chuckles, stepping forward again, eyes searching my face as I press my back into the timber post behind me. "You weren't nearly this mouthy when I saw you last."

Rational thought flees my mind at his proximity.

"Things change." My voice comes out soft and raspy as I soak him in. His imposing frame, the way his Adam's apple bobs in his throat as he swallows. Suddenly I feel very young and very out of my depth. I squeeze my thighs together, noting that telltale spark at the base of my spine, that deep thrum in my pelvis.

"They do." Dermot grips my chin firmly and my

breath leaves me in a quick exhale. I stand stock still, chest rising and falling in time with his, not wanting to break whatever tenuous connection we have right now. He places his drink on the porch railing behind me and then trails his index finger over my lips possessively. The top one, and then the bottom one as he muses, "You're too young for me."

I swallow audibly in response, and smirk with a confidence I don't feel. "Guess that makes you too old for me, something you've made very clear now."

His intelligent eyes dart around my face, analyzing me. Like he's making a tactical calculation. "I'm not sure I made myself all that clear, actually." He leans towards my ear to whisper, "Not very clear at fucking all."

I can feel the hard points of my nipples rasping against my bra as his toned body moves in, completely invading my space. His chest presses against mine as we face off, making me feel competitive. Or cornered. Like I want to lash out at him. "What the hell is that supposed to mean?"

"It means nothing should ever happen between us. It would be a mistake."

Good god. This man gives me whiplash.

"Thanks for clearing that up," I spit out. "Now get your hands off—"

"And yet..." He cuts me off abruptly, his hold on my chin tightening as he does. "Fuck it."

His lips crash down onto mine and this time he moves against me almost frantically. Hungrily. I moan into his mouth, trying to kiss him back, but he just holds my head in place, taking what he wants. What he *needs*. The kiss is brutal, primal, like a punishment more than a reward. Like a volcano that's been waiting to erupt. And this lava? It's probably going to burn us both.

But I must have a death wish because I arch my back towards him, pressing into his hard chest. I fist his shirt, wanting to pull him even closer. Wanting to crawl into his embrace and never leave, wanting to memorize the feel of his arms around me and the clean soap smell on his skin. The taste of whiskey on his tongue and the rasp of his stubble against my skin is a combination I'll never forget.

His kisses turn languid, reverent almost, as he cups my head and trails his thumbs over my cheeks. His mouth moves in their wake, peppering kisses over my earlobe, into the crook of my neck, and across the base of my throat. Shooting arousal straight between my legs. I turn to putty in his arms.

This. *This* is what I've spent years dreaming about. But no dream could do the real thing justice. Dermot Harding is powerful, exacting in every touch, experienced in a way I hadn't anticipated; in a way that makes jealous feelings bubble to the surface as his hands roam my body and his mouth lays claim to mine. You don't learn how to own a woman this way without an awful lot of practice. He just hadn't wanted to practice with me.

The realization is like a cold bucket of water over my head. Everything that was molten and hot quickly turns to brittle stone.

I freeze in his arms and panic comes rushing in.

Memories of him turning me away in this exact spot—
something I refuse to feel again. He tries to pull me back
in, resting his forehead against mine. "Ada..." His lashes
flutter shut, and he shakes his head. "What am I going to
do with you?"

His eyes bore down on mine, burning with need as he
rocks into me. I can feel his hard length through his jeans
against my hipbone, a torturous teaser of what I could
have had. Of what I want.

"Nothing." I almost don't recognize my own voice, so
cold it's downright arctic. But what I do recognize is the
survival instinct flaring inside of me. Doing *this* with
Dermot is dangerous for my heart. Maybe it's easy for
him to walk away and waltz back in. But for me? This is
torture. Borderline cruel.

He sighs and steps away from me, almost trembling
with the self-control it takes. "I'm sorry, Ada." His eyes
are earnest and gentle as the heat of his body leaks away
from mine. "This is just..." His hands rest on his hips and
he looks towards the sky, as though he might find guid-
ance up there. "I don't know how to explain what I'm
feeling. I don't know if I should—if I can." He laughs
sadly. "It's been three years and I still can't make sense of
it myself."

His voice is kind, but his words feel like the cruel lash
of a whip. I can't believe we're here *again*. Except this
time, it's worse. This time he kissed me back, practically
knocked me over with the weight of his desire. This time
I know the feelings aren't one sided. And him pushing
me away now because he's too scared to talk to me? It

teaches me something I never knew about Dermot Harding.

I spew venom, not the shy teenager I was last time this happened. "Never took you for a coward, Dermot."

I know my blow lands with force because I see the hurt in the depths of his dark eyes. I feel bad for him momentarily until the humiliation hits. I spin on my heel, needing to get away from him and whatever the hell that just was.

Away from that goddamn porch.

———

I AVOID Dermot the next day, opting not to do any work with Penny. I sulk around the house and offer to help my mom with prepping dinner. Which seems like a great way to clear my mind until she says, "Oh perfect! I could use some extra hands. Your father invited Dermot for dinner tonight so we can catch up with him."

Great, just what I need right now. I can't even bring myself to respond.

"Nice to have Dermot back, isn't it? I hear he's been a big help with Penny," she supplies light heartedly, trying to stir some response out of me.

I just grunt.

"You always had the sweetest little crush on him as a girl. Like his shadow around this place." She chuckles good-naturedly, "I think you'd have followed him to the ends of the earth for a while there."

"Sounds creepy," I mutter, not looking up from the tomatoes I'm dicing.

"Awe, no." A wistful smile touches my mom's round face, and her eyes glaze over as she recalls the past. "Dermot was a good boy then, and he's a good man now. One of the best I've known. I think you could sense that even as a little girl."

I feel an aching twinge in my chest because as much as I want to throw this tomato at his stupid handsome face right now, I know she's right. Sighing, I let my shoulders fall on an exhale. "I know, Mom. He's been a big help with Penny. I think we're going to head out into the fields and gallop next week. See if I can stay on." I wink at her, trying to prove that I'm not sulking as bad as it might seem. Plus, everyone seems very amused by how often Penny has turfed me.

She claps excitedly, so genuine in her response. "I just know you're going to do great things with that little spitfire. She's the start of something new and exciting for you. I can feel it in my bones."

We sit around the dinner table that night making small talk. My parents love having Dermot around, they've always had a soft spot for him. I know they took him under their wing when he had no one else around. I also know they'd have had more children—they'd have filled this whole place up with a herd of Wilsons to take over the ranch for them one day.

Instead, they got me. Just me. One girl who has no interest in cattle ranching. But they don't care, they just want me to be happy. My cheek quirks in amusement.

It's an ongoing joke that maybe I'll marry a rancher to keep the tradition alive. My dad says it and then winks. Yes, Thomas Wilson knows he broke the mold with me, and he loves me for it.

"So, Dermot," my dad starts in, "what are your plans for your land? Do you have anything going on up there?"

"I'm not sure, sir. A company that wants to buy it contacted me, actually. They seem to think the area is rich in mining resources. But I don't think I can bring myself to sell the family farm, no matter what's on that land."

My father stares down at his plate, spearing a piece of chicken and chewing exaggeratedly, like he's really mulling something over. "Don't sell it, son." He sits up and looks at Dermot seated across from him, next to my mother. "That land is valuable, and if they're out hounding you about it, they know there's something good on there. Might be the perfect opportunity for you start something for yourself."

Dermot looks genuinely shocked, like starting his own business isn't something he's ever considered. His dark, heavy lashes flutter across his cheek bones rapidly as he tries to process what my dad has just said to him. "I—"

Tom holds a hand up to stop him. "Just think about it. You know that Lynette and I want to see you succeed. As much as I love having you down here every summer to start my young stock, I also know you're destined for bigger things. You've been through a lot, so if we can help you in any way—connections, financials, whatever—you just say the word. We'd be happy to help."

He looks at my mother now and she nods her head in agreement, eyes shining with emotion. An unspoken agreement, like they know each other so well there's no need to use words. That the two of them still look at each other like this after thirty years never fails to blow my mind. It used to gross me out, but I've come to realize how special what my parents have is. How precious.

I want that.

When I look back at Dermot, he's pressing his lips together, assessing my dad. His voice is rough, full of emotion, when he looks down shyly and says, "I'll look into it. Thank you, Tom. But first I'm helping Ada get that filly to the races."

I pipe up now, excited by the prospect of his help. Because past drama aside, Dermot is one of the best horsemen I've ever met. His help would be invaluable. "Really? You promise?"

He stares back at me sincerely, quieting the room with the intensity of his look. He nods once, decisively. "I promise."

"Good!" My dad barks, breaking the spell. He tosses his napkin down on his plate and leans back in his chair as he turns towards where I'm sitting beside him, like he's totally oblivious to the current between Dermot and I. "So, Ada, what are your plans for Saturday night in Ruby Creek? You going to paint the town red?" He winks.

I know that *moping and drawing hearts with mine and Dermot's initials in them* isn't an appropriate answer.

But really, I have no plans. Which sounds far too lame to say out loud in front of everyone. Why couldn't he have just let me skulk upstairs after dinner without flinging me into the spotlight? Sitting across from Dermot, watching his easy smiles, his hands flexing as he cuts through his chicken, his softly mussed hair flopping across his forehead—this entire dinner has been torture enough.

I suppose that's why I blurt out, "Probably going to head into town for a drink or something."

"With who?" *Why is he doing this?*

I bulge my eyes in agitation. "I don't know, Dad. There's almost always someone there who I know. It's a small town, I'm not too worried about it."

He just grunts in response and I look down, fiddling with the edge of the tablecloth in my lap. Dad's obviously not wild about the idea of his little girl going to the bar by herself for no good reason. I wish I could tell him I don't really want to go either, but now I've backed myself into a corner.

"I'll go with her." My head snaps up. Dermot just shrugs casually, not looking at me. "I could use a little civilization. Haven't been out much since I got back."

"I don't need a chaperone," I seethe. This is not what I want, and I don't care if I sound like a petulant child. I want to be alone, or at the very least just not anywhere near Dermot.

Lately all he does is make me angry and then horny. It's a terrible combination, and I need some damn space, but he's around every corner, his voice echoes around the stables all day long, I swear I get whiffs of his clove scented aftershave when he's not even nearby. The man is driving me to distraction, which is why I hid out in the house today. I'm fed up with his hot and cold behavior. *I'm over it.*

Or at least I thought I was until he came waltzing back onto the ranch and tossed me right back into the deep end of my obsession.

"Ada..." My mother scolds me, I know she's going to make some comment about manners and me being better than this.

But Dermot cuts her off. "Of course you don't. I'll just give you a ride and then leave you to your devices with your friends."

I just glare at him before shoving my chair back and storming upstairs.

4

DERMOT

ADA PULLS herself up into my cobalt blue pickup, huffing out a breath as she slams the door much harder than necessary. She shoves her seatbelt into the buckle roughly before leaning back and crossing her arms, eyes trained straight out the windshield.

Okay, so she's pissed. Again. I guess I can't blame her. I'm a mess. I've *made* a mess.

"Are you going to drive or just sit there staring at me?" Her tone is biting and her jaw is set stubbornly. She still refuses to turn her eyes my way.

Shaking my head, I shift the truck into reverse, looking over my shoulder as I back out onto the long driveway. "You used to be cute, now you're a mouthy pain in the ass, you know that?"

I swear she almost growls in response. Her mouth purses like she's eaten something sour, the tip of her dishy nose twitches, her chest flares an angry red, and she literally turns her entire body away from me to look out the window. "Good. That's what you deserve."

Her words don't hurt, I'm a grown man. It takes more than a shoot from the hip insult to wound me, but the physical act of her turning away from me, that she can't even look at me—that aches like a rusty lance to the heart.

My poor behavior, my inability to control my urges around her, or really even just communicate, has hurt one of the few women I've ever truly cared about. The woman I've spent the last three years dreaming about, writing letters to that I never had the balls to send. The woman I feel *more* for, but can never pursue.

Agitation blooms within me as I run through the last week in my head. Every time I've put my hands on her body when I should have kept them to myself. All the words that have spilled from my lips, that I should have shoved back down when I felt them bubbling up.

The last thing I ever want is to hurt Ada. Which is why I make a pact with myself, right here and now, as we drive in tense silence along the quiet dirt road.

I need to talk to her. I need to explain. I need to show her the letters so that she doesn't go on thinking that this thing between us is one-sided.

Impossible? Yes. But one sided? Definitely not.

She jumps out of the truck almost before I've put it in park, like the cab is on fire and she can't get far enough away, and takes off through the heavy wood door of Neighbor's Pub. The only watering hole around Ruby Creek.

I sigh heavily as I lock up and then trudge toward the

entryway of a bar I don't really want to be at. I'm tired, I only volunteered to go out tonight because I could see the worry etched on Tom's face over his only daughter going out by herself. And I couldn't blame him, or at least that's what I was going to tell myself.

That's right, I'm only here tonight to do a friend a favor. It has nothing to do with the fact that I'm obsessed with his daughter and can't stand the thought of her out with another man.

Striding into the dark little bar, it takes my eyes a moment to adjust. Ada has already found herself a spot at a table just next to the bar with a few friends. Two guys and one other girl. It gets my hackles up that it looks like they're on a double date now. I have no right to feel this way, and yet I pull out a stool up at the bar, near to the little square table, pathetically hoping that if I listen hard enough bits of their conversation might filter over to where I'm sitting.

That's where one week around Ada Wilson has gotten me, a thirty-one-year-old man. Trying to ignore the frequent boners I get from just watching the way her ass fills out a pair of jeans as she walks around the farm and hoping I can eavesdrop on her conversations with friends. *Pathetic*.

Someone slaps the glossy bar top in front of me and I startle before looking up into the kind, wide face of the man behind the bar. "What can I get ya?"

I clear my throat as I look down the back shelf, full of glass bottles. "Just a beer is good."

The man grabs a pint glass and steps over to the taps,

cranking the handle towards himself to let the golden liquid spill out. He's got a big farm boy build about him, dark blonde hair, I'm willing to bet he's only a year or two older than Ada. "You new around here? Don't think I've met you before." He drops a coaster down in front of me, plunking the frothy beer on top, and then offers me his hand. "Hank Brandt."

I squeeze his hand back. "Dermot Harding. Nice to meet you. I live up near Merritt but come down in the summers to help Tom Wilson with some colt starting."

He claps his hands as he leans against his side of the bar, making himself comfortable. "Right on. The Wilsons are good people."

I glance over at where Ada is sitting, nursing a bottle of beer and staring off into space. Clearly not interested in whatever conversation is happening at her table. "The best," I say absently.

"You bring Ada out tonight?"

I scoff and shift my attention back to Hank. "Yeah. Tom wasn't wild about her coming out alone, so I offered to join. Don't think she much appreciated my offer."

The young man waves his hand dismissively. "No need to worry about Ada. She's a good girl. If a little oblivious."

I quirk my head. "What do you mean?"

His lips tip up and he shrugs his shoulders. "I mean... look at her." I turn to look at her again, and this time she's glaring at me. Trying to incinerate me with her gaze, to burn me to the ground. She might be a good girl, but right now she looks about ready to kill me.

"Every eligible guy in town is interested in Ada, but she doesn't notice. She comes in here, has a polite drink or two with friends, gently turns down offers for dates, and then goes home. I've heard some guys say she's had boyfriends at university, but here at home? I think this is the first time I've ever seen her hang around someone."

"Hm?" I ask as I tip my beer back. The cool fizz spreads across my tongue, soothing the fire I want to breathe at the thought of Ada having plural boyfriends at university.

Hank points. "Travis there,"—my chest tightens—"the one with his arm around her chair. They were in together the other night too."

I sneak a look out of the corner of my eye, and sure enough, the lanky, sandy-haired boy has his arm slung casually over the back of Ada's chair. My first thought is that I want to break his arm, which is swiftly followed by intense shame. Shame that I, for even a moment, would think I have a right to feel that way.

She deserves that. Someone young and vibrant, not brimming with baggage, who can keep up with her and not worry about the implications of his relationship with her. Someone promising and carefree. Unlike me.

I just grunt, hunch myself low over the bar top and take a big swig of my beer. More people filter in around me, and Hank moves on quickly to help the other patrons. I'm grateful to be out from under his assessing stare. The man may be young, but he was looking at me like he had me all figured out. He was making me squirm.

I'm not alone for long, though. A shrill squeal assaults

my eardrum from the same side as Ada's table. "Dermot Harding! Is that really you?"

My body goes rigid as I feel long nails drag across the blades of my shoulders and a body press up against my side. "It is! How are you, honey? It's been too long!"

Tara Bennett, a few-nights fling from just before I left, rubs herself up beside me. "Hi, Tara," I say graciously, "long time no see."

I don't need to look at Ada to know her attention is on me now. I can feel the weight of her stare like a fiery brand on my bare skin. Like a heavy pulse in my bloodstream.

Tara trails her hand over the small of my back and I try not to cringe. What felt good three years ago feels downright wrong now. I turn towards her on my stool so that she's forced to remove her hand. But she just drops it onto my knee and steps towards me. She's wearing a Neighbor's Pub t-shirt with a jean skirt and a black apron. "You working here now?"

"Sure am." She smiles proudly, eyes searching my face excitedly. "I'm off in a couple of hours if you want to catch up. You can buy me a drink." She winks flirtatiously. "For old times' sake. We had some good times, didn't we?" She slides her palm up my thigh boldly, and all I want to do is recoil.

Tara is a pretty girl, no doubt. But all I can think as I stare back at her is that she's not Ada. That's not the face imprinted on the backs of my eyelids. Lips a little too thin, hair a little too blonde, make-up a little too thick, scent a little too sugary. Ada is soft and natural, she smells like the marmalade she has for breakfast every morning mixed with freshly cut grass—that sweet and fresh smell. I love that smell. I love... Don't even think it, Dermot.

The loud screech of a chair against the floor crashes through my awareness. I turn towards the sound, startled, to see Ada shooting up out of her seat. Face bright red like a perfectly ripe apple. Like a poisonous apple.

She marches up to me, swipes my keys off the bar top before I can connect the dots, and storms out the door like a twister on a path of destruction. Through the window, I watch her jump into the driver's seat of my beloved blue truck, crank the ignition, and gun it out of the parking lot. Leaving a spray of gravel behind her while everyone looks on in utter confusion.

Except for me. I'm not confused at all. She just overheard every word Tara said.

5

ADA

I TRY TO SLEEP, but the farmhouse is too hot, my body and mind too restless. The air coming in through my window provides no reprieve and even if I could get comfortable, my overactive brain won't give me any peace. It makes me miss the air conditioning at my university residence hall. I switch the bedside lamp on and look at my clock. *Midnight.*

I heard the crunch of tires on the gravel driveway a couple of hours ago. I heard Dermot when he said, "Thanks for the ride." And as much as I wanted to run to the window to see who drove him home, I was too chicken. I couldn't bring myself to do it. If it was Tara, I didn't want to know. Having to watch her paw him so boldly, so publicly... well, that was more than enough torture for one day. Her suggestive words had been the catalyst for my eruption.

I was ready to scald them both before I decided the safest course of action would be to just leave. And ditch

Dermot. He deserved that. He had to know that letting another woman do that right in front of me would hurt. And I mean *hurt*. The ache in my lungs had been very real. The mental images racing through my mind. God. I'm not sure I'll ever be able to erase them. Suspecting and seeing are two very different things.

I know I'm being immature. Dermot is a grown man, with years of experience on me. Logically, I know it's not like he's been chaste. He's tall, dark, and handsome in the most mouthwatering way. He's funny. He's a perfect gentleman. What woman *wouldn't* turn into a puddle at his feet? But seeing it firsthand was something else. I didn't want to face what his years on me really meant.

Worse than that, I like Tara. Correction: I *liked* Tara. In this moment, I'm not sure I'll ever be able to forgive her for having had a taste of what I want. The unfairness of it burns in my throat and lurches in my stomach.

My fist slams into my soft mattress. I'm far too keyed up to sleep. Too angry. Too *irrational*. I'm tired of feeling like this.

Sighing in frustration, I grab a towel off the back of my door and creep down the creaky old stairs, trying not to wake anyone. I've been doing this for years when I can't sleep. A quick dip in the cool river when it's this hot never fails to help me find peace. I know it's just the mental reset I need right now.

I slide my feet into a pair of sandals and walk across the backyard towards the riverbank, shooting Dermot's laneway house a dirty look as I walk past. The sound of crickets fills the air like a small symphony over the rush of water in the distance. Everything is so perfectly peaceful. It's dark and clear but the moon is full, shining like a spotlight over the entire valley.

I drop my towel in my usual spot. A deep bend in the river where the current is almost nonexistent, where the water is still and deep and cold.

Standing on the towel, I scoot out of my sleep shorts and rip off my tank top, dropping them both on the rocky ground. This is the best part about living in the middle of nowhere—no prying eyes.

I walk to the edge of the water, talking myself into making the plunge. Even though I know how it's going to feel, it takes a lot of internal convincing to throw myself into the icy water, every damn time.

With a small smile, I turn away from the water towards the walls of the riverbank, spread my arms out wide, close my eyes, and fall backwards into the deep pool.

I hold my breath and tread water below the surface, turning myself over to the rush of cold and the breathlessness that follows. The weightlessness of my body and the silty taste of the water that slips past my lips refreshes me. It's peaceful down here; dark and quiet, like time stands still. Like everything about my world is so inconsequential when the river and the rocks around me have been here for centuries. Weathering the storm.

My problems feel like a speck of dust when I think about the vastness and timelessness of the surrounding land.

Noise filters in, warped by the water around me.

"Ada!" I kick my legs towards the surface to see what's going on. "Ada!" The voice is louder as I breach the water. "Ada! Oh my god! Are you okay?"

Dermot is perfectly illuminated by the bright silvery moonlight, calf deep in the water, shirt torn off on the rocky bank, eyes wild and chest heaving like he's about to rescue me. From what, I'm not sure.

I smooth my hair back off of my face as I tread water. "What are you doing, Dermot?" I ask coolly.

He fists his hands on his tapered hips as he regards me, eyes scanning me clinically as if to confirm I'm actually okay. "I was sitting outside, heard a splash." He still sounds out of breath.

I take a moment to admire him, to weigh my response. Where he was still lanky and boyish three years ago, he's filled out now. I let my eyes follow the trails of his defined abdomen, his cut chest, the tempting hollows just above his collarbones, and the way his biceps bunch into a tight ball beneath his broad shoulders. I lick my lips, tasting the earthy river water that's dripping down my face.

Dermot Harding is a boy no more. He's now a clear and present danger to my heart. To my sanity.

"Okay. That doesn't explain what you're doing here." I try to keep my voice even, removed. Wanting him gone. "I'd like some privacy, please."

"You scared me. I thought you were—" He scrubs one broad palm over the dark scruff adorning his jaw. "I don't know. Not thinking straight. In trouble."

My jaw falls open as I realize what he thought I was

doing. Shock, followed by indignant fury. "You think I would kill myself over your dumb ass, Dermot Harding?" I shout breathlessly as I move my limbs beneath the dark water, bringing me closer to the shore, just to where I can touch.

"I—"

"You're an idiot. That's what you are." I scoff before launching back in. "I mean the gall. The absolute gall. Get over yourself."

"I know you're mad about Tara," he says sheepishly, unmoving on the moonlit shore.

I bark out a laugh. "Well, hey, at least you know something. Hope she gave you an eventful ride home."

"What was I supposed to do, Ada? Be rude to a perfectly nice girl? And the bartender drove me back, because *you* stole my truck."

He had me there. The tiny, petty voice in my head wanted him to be rude to her. But I also know he wouldn't be the man I've loved all these years if that was something he'd do. Dermot is brimming with integrity, which unfortunately, I like—even though it keeps biting me in the ass.

"Ugh." I look away, towards the shadowed stand of trees down river, not wanting to meet his eyes. Not wanting him to see how badly I want him. An urge that's only gotten stronger with the more time I spend around him. The beat of a drum that started out quiet and is now so loud I can hardly think over the overwhelming rhythm of it. It isn't fair, wanting something this badly that you can never have.

"That was three years ago, Ada. She means nothing to me."

I think he's trying to be kind, but his comment just angers me instead. "So you can only fuck women who mean nothing to you?"

He doesn't like that comment; his voice changes, and so does his posture. Where before it gentle and coaxing, it's now hard and commanding. "Get out of the water, Ada. You must be freezing. And we need to talk."

I stare back at him, letting the corners of my mouth tug up just slightly as our eyes meet in the dark. I'm not following his orders. "Why don't you come in for a swim, cool off a bit?"

"I don't have a swimsuit," he bites out, voice trembling with barely contained agitation.

I can tell his control is hanging on by a thread. I can almost feel the heat of the fire growing inside of him as I stand there weighing my next move. I can either throw gasoline on that fire, take a chance, push him to the edge. Or I can drench it with cold water and retreat again, preserving my pride.

Maybe it's the heat, maybe it's my exhaustion, but I go for the gasoline.

"Neither do I," I say as I take a deep breath and lay out flat, letting my body float on the surface of the river. Letting the soft white light from the moon illuminate the shape of my body against the black water, letting it highlight the hard points of my nipples and the gentle swell of my breasts that lay exposed for his eyes.

It feels like long minutes drag by as I stare up at the

twinkling stars against the dark blue sky, schooling my breathing, trying to play it cool even though my heart is rioting beneath my ribs. Really, I'm sure it's mere seconds before I hear the steady sloshing of water. Sloshing that fades into quieter swishes before I feel the press of a finger pad on my chin.

"Ada..." The finger trails down the front of my throat gently, like a whisper, pausing momentarily at the dip between my collarbones. I suck in a ragged breath, scared to burst whatever bubble Dermot and I are in right now.

I chance a look at him; the water doesn't come up as high on him and his eyes are locked on my body. Burning across my skin, I swear I can feel the heat of his gaze, the weight of it as he takes me in for the first time. His other palm flattens against the small of my bare back under the water, easily keeping me suspended before him as his finger moves again.

He drags it through the valley between my breasts, sending shots of electricity to my core. Even the cool water between my legs feels like a caress, the way it sways and laps at me under the quiet blanket of night feels downright erotic. Every nerve ending is firing under Dermot's attention.

His lips press together in concentration and I see his jaw tick before his eyes flit up to mine. I can see the desire in his eyes, the indecision. The fire. And it almost knocks me over with its intensity.

It's so obvious. How I ever convinced myself this man didn't want me is beyond my comprehension right now. It's written all over his beautiful face.

His hand flattens and his fingers splay out over the lower curve of my breast. Both of our breathing goes ragged, heavy, and my mind goes blank. It's like all I can hear is our mingled breaths and the rasp of his skin against mine as he palms my breast, squeezing firmly. When he rolls my aching nipple between his thumb and forefinger, I arch up into him, letting my head tip back, like offering myself to him is the most natural thing in the world.

I can't even stop the guttural sigh that tears itself from my throat. Years of longing packaged up in one needy noise.

His hand presses harder into my back as he drops his head to my opposite breast. Latching his lips onto my pebbled nipple while squeezing the other one. *I can't believe this is really happening.* I whimper at the feel of his tongue circling there, before nipping at me—sending a wave of tingling goosebumps across my chest.

I feel hot and wet between my legs as I try to squeeze them together against the ache building there. It's a lost cause, of course, the ache is only starting. It's on the upward trend of a crescendo. If he stops, I'll probably sink to the bottom of this river, devastated and unfulfilled.

But that's all before he slides his lips across my wet skin and cups my cheek possessively. "Do you know why Tara means nothing to me?" he whispers roughly.

"N-no." I stammer out, not wanting to talk about her.

And then he steals my breath with his admission.

"Because no woman has meant a single fucking thing since that night you kissed me."

My heart pounds erratically as I'm lifted out of the water and into his arms. Chest to chest. Pelvis to pelvis. Mouth to mouth.

Dermot's lips claim mine and his fingers dig into my bare thighs as I wrap them around his waist. We pulse together, like one heart beating in tandem. I can feel the erection straining against his wet jeans. I grind my naked sex against the rough denim desperately—wanting more —before tangling my hands in his thick hair and challenging him.

Even if this is just for tonight, I want it all.

"Prove it."

WE CRASH through the front door and tumble into the small laneway house. Dermot's fingers are digging into my ass with the strain of keeping me close while carrying me here from the river. There will probably be bruises tomorrow. I *hope* there are bruises tomorrow.

He doesn't struggle. All that military training is really paying off where carrying me is concerned. "Hang on, Goldilocks," he'd said as he gripped me and marched us back to his quarters.

My mouth hasn't left his skin, I'm going to take my liberties while his hands are busy holding me. The heady scent of his aftershave surrounds me as I trail my tongue over his shoulder and up over the hollow of his throat. He kicks the door shut behind us and groans when I bite down and suck on his neck. *Hard.*

I want to leave a mark.

He turns us and grips my jaw as he pushes my head

back against the door. "Ada, you're playing with fire, showing your teeth like that."

"Good. I want to get burned." I watch his eyes widen and nose flare in the dim light of the small house. I lick my lips, soaking up the dangerous look on his face; he looks almost feral. Wild. Like a man who's lost control.

"I don't want to hurt you." His fingers pulse on my face.

"You already have."

His chest rumbles with a deep growling noise. "I mean with all the things I'm about to do to you. Are you..."

I smirk, knowing he will not like the answer to this question. "You're not the only one who's spent time with people who mean nothing to them. I'm not a little girl anymore, Dermot."

His face darkens and his hips thrust forward into me roughly. Pinning me. "That's done now." He lets go of my chin and looks down between us, where my naked body wraps around him, where he stands between my spread thighs, as he trails his fingers through the folds of my pussy. "This is mine."

I nod my head absently, alarmed by his words but unable to look away from the sight of his fingers on me. I'm entranced.

"Say it, Ada. Tell me you're mine."

My top teeth press into my bottom lip almost painfully as I watch his fingers circling over my aching core. My legs tremble anxiously, but my voice comes out clear and sure. "I'm yours, Dermot. I've always been yours."

My confession seems to be his undoing. He sinks to the floor right where we are, taking me with him. Laying back on the hardwood floors as I hover over him, shock coursing through my system over the fact that this is really happening right now. This man I've longed for— for as long as I can remember—stretched out before me, saying that I'm *his*. It's almost more than I can process.

When he angles his hips up, I grab his wet jeans and drag them down his legs, discarding them beside us, exposing muscular thighs and the outline of his rigid cock straining against the front of his boxers. My tongue darts out as I peel those off too, mouth going dry at the sight of him bobbing before me; impossibly thick and ready.

He's pushed up on his elbows, looking wide eyed and uncertain, cheeks pink with arousal, dark waves disheveled from my fingers. I pause, soaking up every glorious inch of his body. Every line, every scar, every freckle. I want to memorize it all. Stamp it into my mind. I want to remember this moment for the rest of my life.

My chest aches with the beauty of him laid out before me. The sizzling burn of anticipation covering my skin. I push my knuckles to the floor, feeling the bite, wanting to make sure this is real. The words spill breathlessly from my mouth before I can stop them, "I've wanted this for so long."

His length jerks in response and he reaches for his jeans, pulling a condom out of his wallet and offering it to me. "Show me."

Our fingers touch as I take the wrapper, that same electricity I've always felt coursing through my veins like a storm. "I'm on the pill. Are you clean?" He nods once, his eyes wide and honest and totally heart-melting. I can almost feel my anger at him seeping away, dissolved by the droplets of water that are sprinkled around us. The intensity of my desire taking its place. I toss the foil wrapper across the floor and swing one leg over his body to straddle him. "Good. I want to feel you."

He groans and drops his head to the floor with a thud. Hands trailing up over my hipbones to circle my waist. "You're going to be the death of me, Ada Wilson."

Good, I think to myself. *A little taste of your own medicine.* I reach down between us, fisting the smooth, steely length of him. Loving the sensation of it in my palm, feeling supremely powerful, like for once I might have the upper hand in this game of push and pull between us.

I line the swollen head of his bare cock up with my slick entrance. I should be cold, but instead my skin is burning. The feeling of him notched just inside of me sends a tremor down my spine. And after years of waiting, I drop myself down onto him. I impale myself on his girth and tip my head back on a strangled whimper.

"Fuck, Ada. Fuck..." He trails off, sitting straight up and pulling my breasts flush with his chest, the rasp of my nipples against the dusting of hair there has me mewling in his arms. It's all so much. So many emotions. So many sensations. I feel like I'm puffing more and more air into an already overfull balloon, like if I keep going it's going to burst right in my face.

But I don't care, I can't stop.

I circle my hips on him, grinding down, loving feeling the stretch of him inside me. Dermot's big, and I've never felt so deliciously full. He growls against the skin of my neck, the scrape of his stubble only adding to the blend of sensations coursing through my hypersensitive body. His fingers comb through my wet hair roughly, ending in a gentle tug at the base of my skull as he pulls my face right up to his, forcing me to look into his eyes, which somehow feels more personal in this moment than the knowledge that his bare cock is throbbing inside of me.

"Ada..." His thumb brushes reverently across my lips. "Do you have any idea how fucking good you feel? How many nights I've dreamt of this? The months I've spent trying to stay away from you? To convince myself this was all in my head? Fuck." He dips his chin and squeezes his eyes shut. "The things I want to do you..."

Tears spring up in my eyes. This confession... the time away, the years between us, the reasons this can't go anywhere, they all melt away in the wake of his confession. All the years I've spent feeling embarrassed, thinking I was the crazy one.

None of it matters.

Here. Now. Joined with the man I've always wanted. *Always loved.* This is all that matters.

I cup his cheek tenderly and echo his words, "Show me."

And then his lips are on mine, but it's different this

time. It's leisurely and sensual, rather than hard and frantic. Our hands roam and we rock together in a steady rhythm. I feel every ridge and vein as he slides in and out of me, the rasp against my clit just adding to my frenzy with every thrust. My hips ache with the pleasure, that electric ball of tension building at the base of my spine with every thrust, with every brush of his fingers, with every lingering look.

God, the look in his eyes.

I grind down on him harder, moaning into his mouth. Whimpering against his skin. And when I'm bucking and writhing on top of him, lost to the sensations of having him inside of me, he lays down flat. Thumb going straight for my clit, and says, "Ride me, Ada. Come for me."

The words alone are almost enough to do it. I slam myself down on him hard a few times, taking his full length, feeling the bite of it and loving it. His thumb circles lazily, slick with the wetness of my arousal. And suddenly that building ball of tension snaps.

"Dermot!" I cry out as I grind on him harder. A single bead of sweat trickles down between my breasts like an arrow for the hot lance of pleasure surging through me as I ride the waves of my orgasm. And he doesn't stop touching or thrusting as I come apart around him. In fact, he picks up the pace, pushing me even further until my feet cramp and my thighs shake. Relentless in his taking until he joins me with his own release.

I feel him go rigid beneath me and growl possessively as he spills himself inside of me. I feel my heart swell inside my chest, knowing that nothing has ever felt more right.

I fall forward onto his dampened torso, and he pulls me tight against him. Kissing my hair and trailing his hand up and down the indent of my spine. Our breathing is heavy and perfectly in sync, the only sound in the quiet house. I twirl a finger absently in the splash of hair on his chest, suddenly feeling like a little girl who finally gotten the thing she's always wanted.

Speechless. Breathless. Sated.

Overwhelmed.

But that's before Dermot whispers into my ear, "Time for a shower. I'm going to wash every inch of your body. And then I'm going to make a mess of you again."

An excited tremor courses through me, and I smile into his chest. "Let's go get messy then."

———

I FALL BACK into the plushy feather pillows with a satisfied sigh. Dermot has spent the last several hours between my legs in one fashion or another, and I am positively boneless. I can die a happy woman now.

In my fantasies we'd been good together, but this was beyond. The chemistry. His skill. My hunger. It made for better sex than I've dared to dream about. If I'd known it could be like this, I would truly have lost my mind when he turned me down three years ago.

Saved by my own obliviousness.

But then I get to wondering if it would be like this at

all if we hadn't been forced apart. If we hadn't had years to simmer and stew and *imagine*. I still can't believe that he's thought of this with me—that this might not be completely one-sided after all. And if I hadn't tried a thing or two in the dark, under the covers, with inexperienced boys at university, would I even be able to fathom the enormity of the last few hours with this man?

I don't think so.

I reach out to interlace our fingers as we lay beside each other, staring at the ceiling, watching shadows take form across the wood beam ceiling as the early morning light reaches into the room. Snatching the safety and cover of night from us, or at least from him.

"You should get going."

My heart stutters and I go still. "I'm sorry, what?"

He rolls onto his side to look at me, head cradled in his palm. "I just mean back to the main house so that your parents don't find out."

I blink rapidly. Trying to catch up. Trying to wrap my head around what he's saying. "Dermot, I don't care if my parents find out."

He stares down at me intensely, with a sad smile on his face. "Ada... your dad—your parents—they've become friends to me, family almost. Taken me under their wing. Provided me with good, consistent employment. I can't just walk out my door in the morning with their only daughter on my arm. And everyone here, or in the town, what would they think? I've known you since you we're a child. I never thought of you like this until that night on the porch, but no one else will know that."

Dread coils in my stomach. I hate the idea of keeping us a secret. Like there's something dirty about us being together somehow, but I also don't want to scare Dermot off. I need to figure out a way to strike a compromise.

I gaze back at him as I pull the sheet up over my naked body, uncertainty buzzing in my head now. "Okay but are we... is this..." I groan and roll onto my stomach burying my face in the pillows. I hate how I sound even asking, I hate needing him to reassure me that this is *more*.

The heat of his body presses up beside me and I feel the drag of his teeth across my bare shoulder as he pulls the sheet back down. "Don't hide from me, Goldilocks. I told you. You're mine. I just... we need to think about this. I want you to be sure you know what you're getting yourself into with me. I have a hard time believing you'll want me if you realize how fucked up I am."

"Are you talking about when the truck backfired the other day?"

His eyes go distant, to another place, as he carefully mulls my question over. "It's more than that, Ada. I'm not the same man I was when I left. I've seen too much. Been left behind too many times. I don't even think I like this new version of myself."

My heart thuds heavily and my chest aches, struck by the deep sadness in his voice. I don't know what to say to his assessment of himself. I wish he could see himself through my eyes. Strong and patient, with a wicked and addictive mouth. I feel safe when I'm around Dermot and all I know is that I want him any way I can have him.

Walking away after last night would be... I can't even think about it. So instead, I lean into his broad chest and press a kiss right over his heart. "I like every version of you, Dermot Harding."

And then I wrap myself in a sheet and scamper back to the main house.

DERMOT

I'M DRAGGING TODAY. Which is saying something, because I haven't slept a full night since my tour. Usually, colt starting gets my adrenaline pumping; it's exciting to see the young horses get a good foundation. I live for long days on the ranch, it's where I feel most like myself—most at ease. But after a stressful first half of my night followed by a very active second half of the night, all I want to do is crawl back into bed.

With Ada.

There's no denying my feelings for her are real anymore. What I was convinced was merely a broken man's fixation on something innocent and unsullied, a comforting memory, is clearly so much more. I shouldn't have let things go that far, I should have stuck to my plan and kept my distance. Because after last night all my carefully built walls are mere rubble scattered at her feet.

I scoff at myself as I pull the saddle off the tired buckskin colt. I'd crashed through those walls like a god damned bull in a china shop without considering the consequences of our relationship. What would people think of me? A man in his thirties, who's known this girl since she was little. Who's taken a vow of honor, promised to protect people. Now... it feels wrong when I run through the scenario in my head. It feels worse when I consider how betrayed her parents might feel. How her reputation in this small town might suffer.

But when I'm with Ada, everything feels right. Last night my mind felt quiet for the first time since I left the army. With her I wasn't just going through the motions, I was *present.*

And I want that every day. At what cost though?

Since my parents took off, Tom and Lynette have become like family to me. I don't want to lose them. But now I've put myself in an impossible situation. Keep Ada and fess up to her parents—who I love and respect, but who will no doubt want to castrate me. Or give Ada up and... well, I can't even bear the thought of it now.

You are so royally fucked, Dermot.

I give the young quarter horse a light brush before walking him back out to his herd. Taking deep, calming breaths of the warm summer air. Until my eyes land on Ada's jean clad ass, and then the wind is knocked out of me all over again.

She's walking out towards Penny's paddock, spinning the lead rope in her hand and humming tunelessly as she goes. She doesn't look worried at all. And like she can feel my gaze on her, she turns her head back over her shoulder, looking directly at where I'm standing.

I'm immobilized. I just stare back, slack jawed, unable to process the fact that an angel like her would ever choose a damaged man like me. How could she possibly know that she likes every version of me? She saw me crumple that day when the truck went off. How can she possibly throw caution to the wind like that? How can she can forgive me so easily for pushing her away, for breaking her heart? It all seems impossibly naïve on her part. *That's why it's my job to warn her off.*

And how the fuck am I supposed to get anything done with her around when all I want to do is strip her down and bend her over.

She's practically glowing, and the smile she gives me now? It's like looking into the sun—downright blinding.

A hard clap on the back knocks me right out of my daydream, and I try to will the swelling sensation in my jeans away as I turn to face... Tom Wilson.

"Morning, sir." I tip my head nervously, color draining from my face, hoping he didn't notice me ogling his little girl. Hoping he doesn't notice my uncontrollable erection.

"For crying out loud, Dermot. Why do you insist on still calling me sir? It makes me feel old."

I chuckle. "Sorry, Tom."

"That's more like it." He waves me along as he turns to walk back towards the barn. "Tell me how the horses are coming along before I head into town."

I give him a brief rundown of how each horse is doing, assuring him they'll all be broke and safe to sit on by the end of the week.

"You've always had a special way about you, Dermot. The horses know it, and so do people. It's hard not to love you."

My throat drops into my stomach like a stone. *If he only knew what I'd been doing to his daughter last night, he might not feel so sentimental.* "Thanks," I choke out awkwardly, looking away, unable to hold his gaze.

He barks out a laugh as he hops up into his pickup truck. "Hell of a mosquito bite you've got there, kid." I look back at him in confusion, realization only dawning on me when he smirks and taps his neck.

Ada's teeth left a bruise.

———

I'M TRYING to help Ada with Penny, but everything about her is driving me to distraction. The way her breasts bounce while she rides, the way her golden hair trails in the wind behind her when she gallops, the way she swung her leg over the saddle like she's swung it over me last night.

Essentially, I'm a horny mess who can't stop envisioning all the ways I could corrupt a perfectly sweet twenty-one-year-old girl. *I want to corrupt her and only her for the rest of my life.*

Which is an alarming thought, a monumental realization, and truthfully more than I'm equipped to deal with.

"We galloped!" Ada singsongs from ahead of me as she slides down Penny's sweat slicked flank, her entire body vibrating with contagious excitement.

My boots hit the ground as I step down off of Solar, grinning back at her. "You look excited."

Her emerald eyes rake down over my body suggestively and one eyebrow quirks up when she gets past my oval belt buckle. My body won't stop reacting to her mere proximity, no matter how much my brain begs it to stop. "So do you."

"Not here, Ada." I chide her, turning away, not wanting to hurt her feelings. But also not wanting to get caught by the other staff that are around the ranch. I hate that I have no control where she's concerned. I thought if I waited a few months after getting home, that if I could force myself to stay away from Gold Rush Ranch even though it was only a couple of hours away, that I'd be able to resist her draw—the imaginary connection I'd built up in my head overseas.

I didn't even last a full week. And god knows I hadn't kept my hands to myself in the days leading up to last night either. For a soldier, my self-control is truly atrocious.

Back in the barn, we tie up and untack our horses silently. There's an unspoken tension between us. I know Ada doesn't understand my resistance and I can see the agitation in her every movement as she takes care of her little red mare. Even Penny seems nervous in Ada's presence. Like she can feel the storm brewing beneath her innocent-looking exterior.

We're walking past the hay shed after turning the horses out when she unexpectedly grabs me by the elbow and drags me into the darkened building. Before I can even protest, she's fallen to her knees and is grappling with my belt buckle, yanking my jeans down and fisting my cock like she's out for revenge.

"Ada—"

"Shut up, Dermot. I don't want to hear your excuses. Being around you has always been painful, but being around you and knowing what it's like to have you? It's downright unbearable."

She flattens her tongue, licking the head of my cock like a lollipop, and my mind goes blank. All my rational reasons to protest what she's doing fly right out the window. My hips buck towards her face when she wraps her lips around my girth, and when she slides her head towards my pelvis, I grab hold of the old plywood wall beside me to keep myself upright. Her tongue swirls and her cheeks hollow out as she works me, running her hands up over my thighs, squeezing my ass. Rolling my balls in her petite hand until I feel like I might lose control and finish right here and now.

But I'm not done. As much as I'm enjoying this, I want more.

I fist a chunk of her hair and pull her off of me, revelling in the way her eyes go wide and her lashes flutter as she looks up at me from the dirt floor of the shed. Reaching down, I scoop her up and turn around, sitting her on a stack of square bales as she squeals in surprise.

"Three bales high, the perfect height to taste what's between these thighs."

"Oh god." Her cheeks are stained the prettiest pink as

she shimmies her hips to help me get her skin-tight jeans pulled off.

I toss them to the ground but put her beautifully stitched leather boots back on. "This is a good look for you, Ada," I murmur as I take hold of her thighs and spread her open before me. "You look fucking edible."

Her only response is the silent parting of her lips in the sweetest little O-shape. She may have experimented with other men, but I can tell she doesn't have that much experience and I am thriving off the quiet but needy way she reacts to me. I like that I can shock her with my mouth, and I know she does too as I watch her body tremble under my gaze.

I swipe a thumb through her folds and watch it come back glistening. I pop it into my mouth with an audible, "Mmm," as I taste her, watching her eyes go wide and doe-like in response. "Tastes like..." I lift her legs higher before I growl, "mine."

And then I dive in. Starting off slow and gentle with my tongue but ending up hard and fast. Urged on by her writhing and moaning, by her fingers raking through my hair.

Her legs shake, and she clamps them around my neck, but I don't stop. I add a finger, sliding into her wet heat while I continue to work her with my tongue. "Oh my god, Dermot. Please don't stop," she murmurs as I coax the orgasm from her body.

When it hits, her back arches and her hands turn to fists in my hair, yanking rhythmically, lost to her own pleasure. And I grin, loving making her fall apart like this. For me.

"Thank you," she sighs, breathlessly.

I pull away and quirk an eyebrow at her. "Oh baby, I'm not done with you yet."

She just smiles as I pull her down off the stack of hay bales. Grabbing the twine of the top one, I chuck it onto the ground beside us and then spin her around. One hand on her hip and the other flat between her shoulder blades, I lean forward and whisper into her ear. "Two bales high, the perfect height to bend you over."

She moans as I press her chest down onto the bale of hay and add, "Legs wide, honey." I watch her step each boot clad foot further apart, loving her eagerness. Groaning at how she looks bent over, bare legs disappearing into in her boots.

It's fucking criminal.

I lean over her back while lining myself up, feeling her flutter against the contact. "You love this, don't you, Ada?"

And I slide into her.

"Yes!" she cries out, clenching around my girth and rocking her hips back towards me.

I tut at her playfully as I pull all the way back out. "Needy girl," I growl as I slide back in to the hilt. Pumping into her with a steady rhythm now, hearing my thighs slap against her bare ass, smelling the musky hay around us in the quiet shed, feeling her soft body moving beneath mine.

This—us—it's everything.

I stand up tall to watch from above and am struck by the depth of my feelings for her. By the enormity of them. How they've crept into my mind over the years no matter how hard I've tried to keep them at bay. I grip her hips, thrusting harder, driven wild by the fact that this woman wants *me,* when she could pick any man in the world. My control has gone up in a puff of smoke where she's concerned. And in this moment, I don't even care.

When she spasms and cries out my name beneath me, a blush spreading across her lower back, hitting that high for the second time, it's almost more that I can take. And knowing that she's been taken care of means I can chase my release with abandon.

"My turn," I say gruffly, just as sensations and emotions collide, shoving me right over the edge after her. As the tension between us ebbs, I lean back down to cover her body with mine, to press a kiss just below her ear. To tell her we're going to make this work. That I'm *never* going to give her up.

But then I freeze. The shed door swings open, and a voice growls through what was previously a private, safe space.

"What the fuck is going on here?"

I scramble to cover Ada. I don't even care that my jeans are around my ankles; she doesn't deserve this. Prying eyes. I recognize the voice as one of the farm hands, Gord. It's not news to me that these guys are ultra-protective of Ada, they always have been. But being righteous enough to announce yourself this way takes some serious balls.

I know I'm in trouble.

"Get out!" I bark angrily. Mind spinning with what this means for me. For her. For *us*.

When I hear the door close, I stand up and mutter, "Fuck!"

Ada stands and spins to face me, reaching for her jeans. She's still flushed from her orgasm, but her eyes are wide and alarmed. She rubs my arms as I do up my pants. "It's okay, it's okay..."

"No, Ada. It's not," I scrub a hand over my face. "If he tells anyone before I get a chance to explain... You don't understand."

"Explain it to me then."

"I've been around here as an adult since you were a lanky little kid with a rat's nest for hair. The things they'll say about us... People won't understand that I never thought of you this way even once until that damn kiss." I rake my hands through my hair and look up at corrugated the tin roof.

She tips her chin down to button her jeans before hitting me with the most innocent, trusting look. Like a shot to the heart. "We're both adults now, Dermot. Who cares what people will say?"

"Your parents are more than just friends to me, they're the family I never had. My own took off and haven't come back to see me. I can't do this to them. Disappoint them like this."

"Why would making me happy disappoint them?" She sounds genuinely confused.

I knew this would happen. I knew this was a bad

idea. I've known all along that I should stay away from Ada Wilson. That giving in to my confused and fucked up daydreams borne of an innocent kiss years ago would only lead to trouble. I should have been stronger, because now this will hurt more than just me.

I grasp her face and kiss her forehead reverently before turning and walking out of the shed. If Ada doesn't care about her reputation—her future—I'll have to be the one to do it for her.

Gord's leaning up against the far corner of the build-ing, a big wad of tobacco tucked into his lip, picking at his nails. He barely spares me a glance as I walk up. "The way I see it, one of us tells him or you just hop in that truck and head back up to the mountains."

I sigh. Hating the decision, but refusing to be the thing that messes Ada's life up. I can give up the Wilsons if it means that Ada gets to go on and live life without a black mark against her name.

"I'll leave.

I RUSH UP towards the old farmhouse, looking for Dermot. Needing to find him. That kiss on the forehead felt different. It lacked the heat and grit of our past several interactions.

It felt like goodbye.

He finally comes into view, jogging down the front steps of my parents' house. His shoulders are tense and tall as he marches across the driveway, that military training peeking out like it does sometimes now.

"What are you doing?" I ask, dread coiling in my gut. It's like my body already knows what my mind refuses to accept.

"I just went to let your mom know that I'm leaving. She'll pass the message on to your dad." He continues walking right past me, towards the little laneway house. Alarm bells ring in my ears.

"Where are you going?"

"Back home, up to Merritt."

I chase after him, like a sad little puppy on his heels. "For how long?"

He swings the front door open and I follow him through before he finally turns to look at me. His eyes are all steel. Cold and determined. The way he looked at me the night before, while I straddled him, right in this exact spot? All that warmth is gone.

"For as long as it takes." His words are like ice on my skin.

"For as long as *what* takes?"

"Sorting myself out. I can't do this to you." I gasp, but he just turns and starts shoving stuff into his duffel bag.

"Seriously, Dermot?" Anger bleeds into my voice, making it wobble. "You're going to run again?"

"I didn't run, Ada. I joined the army, served my country. Learned some tough lessons about life and myself. It's time you did the same."

"Oh yeah? Tell me, Dermot, what lessons am I supposed to be learning right now?" I cross my arms, digging my nails into my skin so hard it will leave marks.

He looks up at me. Dark eyes boring into mine, not unkindly, as he says, "That girlhood crushes are just that. Best left in the past."

I rear back as though he's just slapped me. This man made love to me, right here, last night. And now all of that is just a girlhood crush? I'm speechless. Frozen. All I want is for the floor to open right here and swallow me whole, but he continues talking as he drops his bag by the door and straightens the kitchen.

"I'm too old for you, Ada. I'm too broken. I've never

had a long-term relationship, don't even know if I can manage one. I haven't slept through the night even once in almost three years. Loud noises scare me. I've seen things I can't get out of my head. I'm a mess, and you have the entire world in the palm of your hand. You deserve so much better than to be stuck limping along with me." His voice cracks with emotion and he tips his head up to stare at the ceiling.

My chest aches, the kind of ache that shoots right into my throat and threatens to transform into that all-consuming type of nausea. My cheeks feel hot and my eyes sting, but I refuse to cry. Dermot doesn't need me to feel bad for him. He needs a swift kick in the ass.

My finger shakes as I lift my hand to point at him accusingly. My voice comes out steely and eerily calm. An absolute bluff. "I have a dad, Dermot. He teaches me lessons, not you. You're just an asshole who's too self-absorbed to realize what he's got staring him in the face. You'll never be happy because you're too busy feeling sorry for yourself."

His jaw ticks, like he's swallowing words he wants to say. I hope the taste of the apology he owes me is bitter. I hope it turns his stomach.

"You should go," is all he manages to bite out.

The finality of his words land like the lash of a whip. I try not to flinch, but I fail.

"So should you," I say, turning on my heel and storming out of the house.

I've been here before. I should have known better.

————

I DON'T WANT to face my parents and I don't want to face the staff. So I go to the only place where I know for a fact I won't face any judgement: Penny's field.

I duck through the wooden fence and head towards where she's grazing. The summer sun is beating down on her slender back, and her tail is swishing back and forth, keeping any bugs at bay. She looks shiny and healthy, bright copper—like a brand new penny.

She's come along so quickly with Dermot's help, and the realization that I'll always have to attribute some of her progress to him stings like whiskey on an open wound. There's not a single place, or thing, on this farm that won't forever remind me of him. This is *my* home, *my* safe haven. And he waltzed in and stomped all over it. *Again.*

How could I have been so gullible?

I get close enough that Penny's head snaps up. She knickers her greeting; wide, intelligent eyes blinking back at me innocently—like I don't already know that this little chestnut mare has a devilish streak. I smile at her sadly. I like her sassy side; I wish I could be more like her. Tougher.

Because right now, I feel downright fragile.

And when I finally run my hands up around her silky neck, when I feel her warm, damp exhale on my shoulder, my carefully curated game-face melts. The ache in my chest breaking through every barrier I've erected, hitting me with full force.

Taking my breath away as I burrow my face in the filly's neck and break down.

I don't know how long I stand there crying. But Penny's patience with me wears out, and she eventually steps away, a wet spot on her neck, to get back to her grass.

I don't know what to do. I feel like I'm living in a waking nightmare. The sky is perfectly blue, the fields are bright green, the birds are chirping happily, and yet my world is crashing down around me. How can such a perfectly pretty day feel so utterly ugly?

How did I come so close to having everything I've ever wanted, only to be left here with nothing in the blink of any eye? How was I supposed to come back from knowing what having him felt like?

I plunk down on the grass, laying out flat, feeling too dizzy to go anywhere else, finding the sound of Penny's teeth ripping at the grass to be rather soothing. The puffy white clouds above me float peacefully, and I'm taken back to my days as a child on the ranch. Playing in the dirt all day long, jumping onto horses with no saddle or bridle, cloud gazing and daydreaming of Dermot Harding. I'm pretty sure I even pulled petals off of daisies. *He loves me, he loves me not, he loves me...*

Now all I see in the clouds are white, meaningless blobs. A manic giggle erupts from my chest. Talk about a grim outlook for a twenty-one-year-old woman with her entire life ahead of her.

"Should I be worried about you?"

My dad's voice wraps around me like a warm hug. I

hear him give Penny his signature loud pats on her muscled shoulder. "No."

"Ada, you're lying sprawled out in the field, staring at the sky, laughing. I've been watching you, I don't even think you've blinked. I love you, but this is creepy."

I smile at the image he just painted. It is pretty creepy when he puts it like that. "Love you too, Dad," is all I can think to say back right now.

"Your mom's been looking for you. It's dinnertime." How could it be dinner time? How long have I been lying here for?

"Oh, sorry," I mumble, still fixating on the fact that I've been lying in the field for hours now.

He mumbles something that sounds an awful lot like, "I'll fucking kill him," before taking a seat on the ground beside me.

He picks up a blade of grass, eyes it warily, and then places it in the corner of his mouth. A rancher through and through. "You alright, my girl?" he asks without looking at me.

I sigh. I don't want to lie to my dad, he's been a pillar of support in my life. My biggest fan. I don't want to think he'd be disappointed in me now. But Dermot has planted a seed of doubt with the intensity of his shame. Maybe I'm out to lunch. Maybe he's right.

So I settle on something truthful that also gives nothing away. "I will be."

He just grunts and picks at the soil between us.

"Of course you will. You're my daughter."

DERMOT

I'VE ALWAYS FOUND the mountains that surround my family farm to be oppressive. But these past two weeks they've become downright depressing. Too tall, casting too long of a shadow, and way too fucking cold.

I miss the warm sunshine and rolling hills in Ruby Creek. I miss the camaraderie of being around other people at Gold Rush Ranch.

I miss Ada.

The further I drove away from her, the less my reasons for leaving seemed to make sense. Last time I *had* to leave. The army was waiting for me. But now? There is absolutely nothing waiting for me. An empty farm and a traumatized mind are all I have for company.

With nothing else on the horizon, I finally got an independent geologist out to check my land for mining deposits. It appears I've hit the literal gold mine in that department. My reward for being the last Harding standing on this farm. When everyone else had the good sense to leave and start something new, I hunkered down. Too sentimental to part with it.

Too sentimental to do anything—to even move, apparently. Which is why I've spent my last several days walking and mapping the perimeters of my land. Checking the fences in the morning and then sitting on the front porch of the rundown house, staring out at my land in the afternoon. With over 80,000 acres, I should be able to keep busy for a while.

The cows are long gone, sold before I left on tour. The chickens, too. No crops to speak of. The only signs of life here are the wildlife that passes through, the wildflowers that have taken over the valleys in my absence, and the squirrels who I'm pretty sure are now living in the attic.

And me. But I'm not living. I'm going through the motions. I sleep in fits and starts, often woken up by flashes of my time overseas—but that's not new. What is new is being woken up by deep regret over leaving Ada, rather than sweet dreams about one innocent kiss.

The memory of what we could have had under different circumstances haunts me. The way her ears went red and the tip of her nose twitched to hold back the tears when I'd told her I was leaving again.

The way I'd held her heart in my hand and crushed it up into dust. All because I'm too big of a coward to fess up about how I feel and face whatever the repercussions might be. And maybe even more so because I'm fucking terrified to need anyone who might leave me. Who might move on. Everything about every person in my life has been so impermanent. My parents, my older siblings, the friends I made in the army. Why would it be any different with Ada?

She's young. She's at university. I know she's going to run a racehorse business one day; I know it in my bones. Because Ada Wilson is smart, and strong, and an absolute go-getter. The last thing she needs is a broken-down man holding her back.

This is the best course of action for both of us. Even if it doesn't feel that way right now. Or at least that's what I keep telling myself.

I take a deep swig of my beer and rest my head on the back of the porch swing, giving it a good shove, hoping that maybe it might rock me off for a few minutes of peace. Where I could let myself remember the feel of Ada's silky skin beneath my fingertips, the press of her tongue into my mouth, the sound of her moans as I move inside her.

This is a good dream.

I can feel myself drifting until the sound of tires rumbling over gravel cuts into my consciousness. Cursing without opening my eyes, I feel my body go rigid. I just want to be alone right now.

When the hum of the engine gets close enough, I open one eyelid.

And when Tom Wilson steps out of his truck, I open both and straighten myself. Alarm coursing through me. *Why the hell would he drive all the way up here?*

I sit up, blinking at him, rubbing my eyes to make sure I'm not seeing anything. His truck is parked beside mine, except he's got a two-horse trailer attached to his, and by the way it's swaying I'm thinking there's probably a horse or two in there as well. I'm so damn confused.

"You look like hell, son," he says good-naturedly as he climbs the steps up to the front porch.

"Wasn't expecting any visitors." My voice cracks after days of not speaking to anyone.

"Wanted to come for a visit. Felt like a trail ride in the mountains." He looks out over my land appreciatively.

I just blink at him in confusion. "You could have called."

He waves me off. "We both know you wouldn't have answered."

I just grunt. *He's not wrong.*

"You gonna offer an old man a beer, or just keep sitting there like a sulking bump on a log?"

"Sorry." I shoot up off the swing, realizing how rude I've been in the wake of his arrival. *Way to welcome a man you profess to love and respect, Dermot.* "Here." I point at the swing. "Take a load off and I'll grab you a cold one."

He gives my shoulder a brief squeeze as I slide past him into the messy house. In the kitchen, I hold the edge of the counter and bow my head, trying to figure out what the hell Tom Wilson is up to. If he knew about Ada and I and was angry with me, well, I couldn't tell. But there's only one way to find out.

With two fresh beers in hand, I step back out onto the

deck. "Beautiful farm you've got up here, Dermot. I can see why you didn't want to let it go."

I hand him his beer and take a seat in the big Adirondack chair across from him. "Seems like I made the right choice."

Tom takes a long pull of his beer and looks back at me inquisitively.

"I did what you said and had somebody out to survey the land, drill some holes and all that."

He leans forward to rest his elbows on his knees, his watery blue eyes regarding me with a knowing look. "And?"

My eyes scan the scrubby, rocky land around us. "We're basically sitting on a goldmine. Seems that big mining company was sniffing around for good reason." I shift my eyes back to Tom. "Thanks for pushing me to look for myself."

His eyes twinkle, and he shakes his head, leaning back to look out at the craggy landscape. "How much?"

"A lot. A metric fuck ton."

"Well, I'll be... what are you going to do with it?"

"Start a business, I suppose. Though I have no idea how to do such a thing." I look up at him, properly meeting his eyes for the first time since he pulled up. "Your offer to help still stand?"

"You've been through a lot for a man your age, Dermot."

I don't respond. What is there to say to that?

"I want to see you succeed. So yeah, of course the

offer still stands. Some start up capital and my support for five percent of the company. What do you say?"

I feel a pinch across the bridge of my nose, a thickness in my throat that I will away. "I don't know why you've always been so good to me."

The sad smile he gives me barely touches his eyes. "Had a soft spot for ya since that first summer you came to work for me. Twenty-years-old and a total idiot. Good with the horses though."

I bark out a laugh. "To be honest, Tom, I'm not sure much has changed. I think I'm more jumbled than I was then."

He just nods at me knowingly, tipping the brown bottle back and swallowing. "Nothing a night out on the range can't fix. Let's pack up and hit the trails so we can set up camp before it gets dark."

"We can just go for a ride in the morning, Tom. We really don't have to do the whole shebang."

He slams his empty beer bottle down on the small table beside him. "You never used to complain about camp-outs. Plus, I can see the inside of your house through the window. I'm too old to sleep in a messy bachelor pad."

I look through the window. Messy doesn't even begin to cover it. I've been a zombie living in a war zone; the place is a disaster. It makes me want to take a match to the old house, burn it to the ground and start fresh.

"Okay, give me ten minutes."

———

I SETTLE in to my sleeping bag, feeling more relaxed than I have in days. Fresh air, a change of scenery, a few sips of whiskey with an old friend. I feel like I'm twenty all over again.

My eyelids feel heavy instantly and under the bright stars, beside the crackling fire, I drift off into a dreamless sleep.

When my eyes finally crack open, it's already light out and Tom is up making coffee over the fire. "Good morning, Sleeping Beauty."

I scrub my hands over my face and sit up, shocked that I slept through the night. "Sorry. I haven't been sleeping much lately."

"How long is lately?" he asks, forehead crinkled in concern.

A ragged sigh pries itself from my chest as I look up at the pillowy clouds drifting in the bright blue sky. "It's probably been almost three years."

"Oh, Dermot..."

I hold a hand up to stop him; I don't want his pity, and I don't deserve it after what I've done to his daughter. "It's okay, Tom. I don't need you to rub my back over it. I'll get better, eventually. It's always worse up here. It's too quiet. Too much time to think about... everything."

"Well, come back down to the ranch then. The laneway house is yours for as long as you need it."

I rake my fingers through my hair, tugging at it in frustration. "I can't."

He pours me a cup of strong black coffee and hands it over. "Why's that?"

"I just..." Shame coils in my gut. *If he only knew.* I take a sip of coffee to fill the silence.

"I know about you and Ada."

And all that coffee gets sprayed out over my sleeping bag as I look at him. One side of his mouth quirks up, but he doesn't look all that amused.

I blurt out the first thing I can think to say. "I'm sorry."

His wise eyes narrow as he takes a deep inhale of his own coffee. "For what?"

"For betraying your trust." My heart is pounding in my chest. Anxiety coursing through my veins. *He's known all this time and acted like we were just going to hang out?*

"The only person you've betrayed is Ada. Me?" Tom lifts his shoulders and then drops them dramatically. "I'm just confused."

I feel my entire face go red. *Betrayed Ada?* Just the combination of the words makes me angry with myself. That's the very last thing I ever wanted to do. "Confused about what?"

"How the man I know could leave behind the woman he loves."

I startle, it feels like he's punched me in the gut. "Did she..." I stare into the inky black liquid in my tin cup. "Did she tell you that?"

Tom just snorts. "You weren't kidding about still being an idiot." We sit in silence for a few moments, both lost in thought before Tom adds, "Any old fool with two eyes can see that you love that girl. And her?" He scoffs, shaking his head in disbelief. "She's always loved you. Right out of the gate. She never stopped. Not even for a minute. And that," he wags his finger at me, "that is a gift most men will never know."

His words hit me like a wrecking ball. They knock the air right out of the valley, like the mountains have finally succeeded in suffocating me. I feel hollow.

"So you... don't care?"

Tom stands and starts packing the camp up, clearly agitated by my line of questioning. "Why? Because you're older than her? Because you've been around for years? I don't care, Dermot! And if you love her like I think you do, what other people think shouldn't matter either!" His voice is quiet, simmering with protective rage as he huffs out a deep, centering breath. "I love you like a son. I want you happy, just like I want Ada happy. And if that's together, then as far as I'm concerned, it's just the best of both worlds."

He shoves our things into bags, obviously done with our camp-out. I hear him mutter something about, "Ya'll are thick as bricks," as I stand to help him silently. Properly chastised.

Our ride back to the house is quiet. But not awkward. Maybe it should be, but I can't help but feel like Tom shed a lot of light on the situation. I also feel like a dog with his tail between his legs, like I should have known better, like I should have trusted myself.

Like I should have trusted Ada.

And now I'm going to have to prove to her she can trust me again. Knowing Ada, it won't be easy.

When we arrive at the homestead, I help Tom pack his trailer up. Years of working together have lent us knowledge of one another, meaning we move around in sync. Getting shit done quietly and efficiently.

When he pulls his truck door open, he turns around to look at me, holding his arms wide. I step into his fatherly hug, feeling his big, comforting slaps against my back—unable to stop the small smile they elicit. This man pats everyone like they're cattle.

When he pushes me back, he looks me dead in the eye, hands on my shoulders. "I can't make personal life decisions for you. But you promised that girl you'd help get her filly to the races. And I know you're a man of your word."

I offer him a decisive nod in response. "See you soon."

I'm going back to Gold Rush Ranch, and I'm going to get the girl whether I deserve her or not.

I REGARD myself in the mirror, making sure my makeup is perfect. Today is the Denman Derby and I'm going to enjoy myself, like I do every year. I've got a new floral print dress on, I've curled my hair and painted my nails—you wouldn't know I'm a total ranch rat unless I told you.

Feeling satisfied with the girl looking back at me, I take a deep breath. "Time to woman up, Ada," I murmur to myself, rolling my shoulders back. "This is your favorite day of the year. Who needs Christmas?"

The girl staring back at me looks beautiful and strong, totally ready to take on the world. And I am. As painful as the last two weeks have been, I've also learned a lot about myself. I feel like I walked through the fire and came out the other side, turned over a new leaf, realigned my vision for my future. I'm sure of myself, of my strength, in a way I never have been.

I think I'll always love Dermot Harding, but I have

other dreams I need to achieve, and I know his dumb ass wouldn't want me to sit around moping. I think I've come to know that Dermot loves me in his own way.

In a way that's not good enough for me.

Because Dermot needs to love himself first. He's so paralyzed by what everyone will think of him, by feeling like nothing is ever permanent, that he can't give himself over to anyone or anything. He's paralyzed.

The realization hit me one night during a midnight swim in the river. He can't put himself first because he doesn't love himself enough to make it a priority. That was the night my tears switched from being for myself to being for him. A man too scared to accept the love I wanted to give him.

An absolute shame. And not something I can fix for him. Lucky for me, I don't suffer from that same insecurity.

So this is the new Ada, forged in fire, soon to be a university graduate and future owner and trainer of Canadian racehorse champions. Dermot Harding had a chance to get on board, and now he can get out of my way.

I trot down the stairs towards the front door, sliding my feet into the strappy heels I picked for today with a small smile on my face. I feel *good*. In fact, I feel great. Until I step out onto the front porch and see a metallic blue pickup in the driveway. Dermot is sitting on the tailgate, swinging his legs, with a bouquet of roses laid across his lap.

His head snaps up at the sound of the door slamming behind me. "Ada—"

Butterflies flap in my stomach, but I cut him off. "No. I don't want to hear it." I march towards my dad's truck as I hear my parents lock up behind me.

"Five minutes, Ada. I brought flowers."

I bark out an incredulous laugh. "Do you know me at all, Dermot Harding? Flowers? Try harder." I pull myself into the back of the cab and slam the door on anything else he has to say. Today is *my* day.

My mom gives him an apologetic pat on his knee and my dad tilts his head and shrugs as if to say, "Women." But within moments, my entire family is loaded up in the truck and Dermot is nothing more than a slouched over figure in the rearview mirror.

———

OUR DAY down at the track is a dream, as usual. The buzz of Derby Day never fails to stir something inside of me. I want to be there, with a horse of my own, running in the Denman Derby. I know now, more than ever, that it's what I'm meant to do with my life.

We had a beautiful dinner, wine, placed some bets— came out even. And now on the drive home we talk about all the horses we saw.

"I want to buy another one, Dad."

"Another what?" he asks, eyes flitting back to me through the rearview mirror.

"Racehorse."

He just chuckles, the apples of his cheeks all round with the width of his grin. "One thing at a time, Ada. Maybe as your graduation present. You only have one year left at university."

I look out the window, into the darkening landscape, and press my lips together to hold back the huge grin threatening to break across my face. I can't wait to get started.

The closer we get to the farm, the more quiet we all become. No one had dared to bring up Dermot's appearance when we drove off, but now the unspoken weight of his arrival is filling up all the empty space in the truck.

"Do you think he's still there?" my mom asks as we turn off the highway.

I just shrug and look away. Probably not. Staying power isn't exactly his forte.

"You know that boy is head over heels in love with you, don't you, Ada?" she presses.

I roll my lips together, trying not to bite back too hard. My mom means well, and I know they both figured out what happened between us too easily for them to not have been onto us before. I knew they wouldn't care. Why couldn't Dermot have just believed me?

"He's not a boy, Mom. He's a grown ass man."

"Ada Wilson! Watch your language!" My mother sounds scandalized, but my dad just laughs. He knows me well.

"It's a fact. He's an adult. And if what you say is true, he's got a funny way of showing it," I add before staring back out the window.

No one can argue with what I've just said. And when we pull up to the house, the truck is dead silent as we peer out into the darkened driveway.

Until my dad groans. Dermot is still here, sitting on the back of his truck. Waiting. It doesn't look like he's moved all day, and even though I just went off about him being an adult... right now? Looking at him? He looks like a lost little boy.

I feel a tug at the center of my sternum, that invisible string that's always drawn me to him, trying to pull me towards him again. The accompanying pinch in my chest makes me want to hug him, to soak up all his pain and disappointment. To lend him my strength.

But I can't yet. I'm still too pissed off. Too hurt. "Don't let him stay here," I say as I hop out of the truck, sniffling. I give him a once over, and then dart into the old farmhouse. Knowing that if I stare at him too long, if I get lost in those dark eyes, my resolve will disintegrate completely. The man is like a big vat of acid for my willpower.

I kick my shoes off and head up to my room to get ready for bed, not wanting to talk to anyone. Ditching my dress, I slip into pajamas and then scrub my face clean until it hurts. I'm about to crawl into bed when I hear the front screen door creak open. I'm up and looking out my window so fast it's embarrassing.

Pulling the lace curtain back ever so slightly, I watch my mom walk out to Dermot's truck with a pillow, a blanket, and a sandwich. *Traitor.* Then I hear her say, "She'll come around." *Double traitor.* She pats his shoulder before she turns to walk into the house and I fall into bed, squeezing my eyes shut hard until I finally drift off into a fitful sleep.

———

WHEN I WAKE up in the morning, I'm dreading looking out my window. If I see Dermot sleeping outside my house, I'm going to fall apart. I wanted him to come back for me, and he did. So why wasn't it enough?

The only thing I can think is the fact that he thought he could just waltz out here with a handful of roses and I'd run back into his arms. It showed a total lack of under-standing—of reflection. The only thing I've ever done with flowers is braid them into my horse's hair.

I drag my feet across the oak floors towards the bath-room but am stopped short by loud metal clanging. *What the hell?*

I pull back the curtain, just like last night. Dermot's truck is still there, but he's moved out into the field next to the barn and is using a mallet hammer on jamming what looks like a bunch of metal fencing together.

I have to admit, he's piqued my curiosity, so I shove on some jeans and head out.

He doesn't look up when I approach the paddock fence. He just keeps working calmly and steadily. I admire him openly, the way his hands flex with each strike, the sweat beading on his forehead. I imagine running my tongue along the bead of it that slips down over his defined cheek bone. And then realizing where my mind has wandered, I start to get antsy with how long he's been ignoring me for.

"What are you doing?" I blurt out, unable to take it any longer.

He just smiles and runs his arm over his forehead, brushing away the perspiration. "Woulda thought you'd recognize this, Goldilocks."

My eyes scan the combination of bars he's put together, but I must be thick because I can't tell what it's supposed to be. "Okay," I huff out, agitated at not being able to pass this test. "Pretend I don't recognize it."

He chuckles, the dimple on his cheek peeking out playfully, and turns back towards his project. "It's a present."

"For what?"

"For you."

I rear back. I know I didn't want flowers, but I'm not sure I want this, either. "Okay... why?"

He comes back to the fence and leans his forearms against it as he regards me. I can't help but look down at the way this position tugs his jeans tight over that very round ass. Being this close to him? It's like being offered water for the first time after spending two weeks in the desert.

He notices. And his cheek twitches, but he has the good sense not to comment. Instead he says, "Because I made you a promise."

I just tilt my head, a silent signal for him to continue.

"To get Penny to the races. This is your new training gate. You only have a couple more months to race her as a two-year-old. And apparently the gate can be a challenge."

I look back at the gate. My mouth is moving, but no sound comes out. *This* is what I was talking about. I don't want flowers. I want *this*.

"Ada, you look like a fish dropped into a dry bucket. Go get your horse. I'm almost done here."

I nod mutely and walk away on wooden legs. What does this mean? Is he only back to help with Penny? Or is he back for me?

I'm standing beside Penny's shiny, coppery coat without even knowing how I really got here. Like my mind has been somewhere else entirely. She drops her head into the halter and we walk back towards Dermot, who is shifting the panels around so it's finally looking like a sort of chute.

"There are more attachments, but apparently the key is to get her comfortable in there. Walking through so she trusts you enough when you eventually box her in."

I raise an eyebrow at him, wondering if he's talking about Penny or me, but carry on anyway. We spend the morning working together. It's torture, feeling him so close to me and yet thinking he might only be back at the ranch on a professional basis. His body heat seeps through my clothes, and his form hovers close to mine as he moves around me, showing me the gate, breaking down how it works, but he never touches me. Not so much as an accidental brush of the leg or nudge of the elbow.

And after a few hours, I'm going insane. I want him

to touch me. Kiss me. Throw me against this stupid gate and have his way with me. My entire body is thrumming with need and he's hardly looked me in the eye.

I know I need to leave. I've embarrassed myself far too many times by throwing myself at this man, and I can't let myself go there again. So I busy myself around the farm and Dermot goes back to sitting on his stupid truck. Like a lost puppy. A sexy lost puppy who I want to kick and then kiss.

When I'm about to head into the house for dinner, I catch sight of him sitting there, casually looking through some sheets of paper, and my patience snaps. I storm towards him. "What are you doing?"

He looks genuinely shocked by the bite in my voice. "I wanted to show you these."

"Not that!" I knock them right out of his hand and watch them flutter to the ground. "I mean *here*. What are you doing here? You gave me the gate. If that's all you wanted, you can now go."

But then I look down and catch sight of the papers near my feet.

Dear Ada...

I bend down and pick up the closest sheet. Feeling the beat of my pulse stronger in my throat.

Dear Ada,

Just got to basic training and everyone here has someone to write to. I'm not sure who else I could send a letter to that might actually want to hear from me, so I guess you're stuck with me.

Yours,

Dermot

P.S. I should have kissed you back.

I look at Dermot, his face completely unreadable where he sits. My hands start to shake and I sink to ground, right on the gravel driveway, desperately grasping at the other loose sheets. *Good god. There are so many.* The papers rattle in my hands as I lift them up.

Dear Ada,

You know that feeling at the end of a long day on the ranch? You've been up early, worked your ass off all day, your legs feel like jelly, and you just crash into bed and have the best sleep? I'm so much more tired than that and I still can't sleep.

Instead, I avoid replaying my days by laying awake thinking about the night you kissed me. Analyzing it every which way I can. Trying to commit it to memory. Why did you do that? Plant a seed in the mind of a man who you knew was leaving? A man who never saw you that way even for a moment? Now I don't know what to think about it, about myself, about you, and I don't even have the balls to ask. It's better this way anyhow.

Yours,

Dermot

P.S. I should have kissed you back.

A ragged whimper bursts out of my chest as I rifle through page after page. Letter after letter. "Dermot..."

Dear Ada,

Everything here is dark, and sad, and depressing. The days blend into each other and the only thing that ties me back to home is you. Your sunny blonde hair, your carefree smiles, the scent of your tangerine body wash that wrapped around me that night when you stood closer than you ever have. The way your hands felt on my shoulders when you leaned in. What I wouldn't give for a simple gentle touch right now.

The longer I'm away, the more I remember things differently. The more I think that maybe there is a connection between us. Is it new? Has it always been there? I don't know. You're so fucking young. You're better off without me.

Yours,

Dermot

P.S. I should have kissed you back.

A tear falls onto the letter in my hands drawing my

attention out of the pages. "Dermot," I say, coming to stand. "I... I never got these letters."

"That's because I didn't send them. Never quite worked up the courage." *All these letters. All this time...*

His jaw ticks as his eyes sear across my body, pausing momentarily on my heaving chest before moving back up to my face. "That's not all I wanted, to give you the gate I mean."

I come back to standing and hold the pages out wide in tearful exasperation. "Then for crying out loud, Dermot, use your words and tell me what you want."

He doesn't even hesitate. "I want you. I want us. I'll sleep in this truck for as long as it takes. If I'm relegated to being your assistant trainer for the foreseeable future, I don't even care. I just want to see you succeed, to see all your dreams realized. And I'll do anything in my power to make that happen for you. I'll love you even if you don't love me back."

My heart riots in my chest. Almost ready to burst with years of unspoken truths and unfulfilled wishes. I almost can't believe what I'm hearing. *Did he just say he loves me?*

I step in closer to him, grasping his knee with both hands and looking up into the depths of his chocolate eyes. "You're a fool, Dermot Harding." The muscles in his thigh tense beneath the tips of my fingers. "Don't you know?" I say more quietly now, feeling him lean down closer to hear what I'm about to say, his breath fanning across the sensitive skin below my ear. "I can't remember a time in my life when I haven't loved you. It's always been you."

Dermot's throat bobs with emotion as one calloused hand comes up to stroke my cheek. I see his eyes sparkle in the late summer sun as a secret smile touches his shapely lips. Lips that are moving closer to mine, lips that I can't wait to feel against my own again.

So I stand up on my tippy toes and kiss him as his broad frame leans down over me, as he grips my head possessively, protectively. We kiss and the world stands still, everything feels so suddenly right. So hopelessly fated. Like no matter what either of us did, we'd have ended up here, today, in each other's arms.

I'm breathless when he pulls back and smiles at me, his thumb stroking my cheek softly. "I'm never leaving you again. If you'll let me, I'm moving into the laneway house."

I just wink through the tears spilling over my lashes, my voice tearful but happy. "I'll think about it."

———

MUCH LATER THAT NIGHT, we lay out in the bed of his truck on a blanket. For the last hour I've made Dermot read me his letters out loud. I've cried, we've kissed, he even stopped at one point to strip me down and show me how much he loves me. And now I'm tucked safely under his arm with my legs slung over his as we look up at the stars. They shine like a string of twinkle lights over the farm, not at all diluted by the glow of the city. It's almost like looking at a painting, never quite the same depending on the day. And today there's a meteor shower.

"Right there." Dermot's hand shoots up to point out the falling star. "Make a wish, Ada."

An airy laugh floats out from my lips as I snuggle in closer. "What am I supposed to wish for? I have everything I've ever wanted."

He presses a sweet kiss to my temple and whispers, "Pick something."

"Okay. I want to win the Denman Derby. I want to win it all. Maybe even the Northern Crown. Doesn't that sound crazy?" I shake my head, grinning.

"No, Ada. It doesn't."

"Oh yeah? You going to promise to make that happen too?" I laugh, nudging his ribs with my elbow, thinking he'll laugh along with me and my lofty dreams.

But instead, he's completely sincere when he looks down at me and says, "I promise."

Then his lips find mine, and I know deep in my bones that the world has a funny way of making wishes come true.

EPILOGUE
DERMOT

BELLS RING and the horses surge out of the gate. I feel Ada's nails digging into the palm of my hand. Her entire body is vibrating with anticipation—with nervousness.

This is Lucky Penny's debut race, and we both know we're out of our league. Two country bumpkins pulling up with one lone little racehorse. But everyone has to start somewhere, and Ada is determined.

Tom had to call in some pretty serious favors to convince a jockey to take the ride on Penny. But here we are, close to the end of the season, watching her blaze across the dirt track in the black and gold Gold Rush Ranch silks that Ada had made. I wrap my opposite hand over the top of hers, feeling the center stone of the ring I put there a week ago dig into my palm. She smiles faintly but doesn't tear her eyes away from the track.

Ada and I happened fast, and yet we didn't. We both had three long years to be sure about one another. And when you know, you know. I wanted Ada, and I wasn't about to wait any longer. Or give her time to come to her senses and pick someone better. We're planning a spring wedding at the ranch, and her parents are over the moon.

Almost as over the moon as when I showed Tom his five percent ownership contract for Gold Rush Resources. I swear the grizzled old rancher teared up at me extending the name of his beloved ranch to our new venture. Ada had rolled her eyes, but I didn't miss the way she wiped at her them either.

"Oh god." Her voice is shrill, snapping my attention back out to the track. Penny is in the middle of the pack but is slowly losing position. Her ears are flicking all over the place. The poor little thing looks nervous. Most racehorses end up living at the track during the season, so the competition is desensitized to the sights and sounds here today in a way that Penny isn't.

But we knew all this coming in. Ada doesn't care if Penny wins, she just loves that lanky, sassy mare and everything she represents. The catalyst that brought us together on more than one occasion. Our very own lucky penny.

"Dermot," Ada laughs, "I don't think we're going to win." Her voice is light and amused, and she's shaking her head lovingly as she watches Penny fall to the very back of the pack.

I pull her into my side, hugging her and dropping a kiss on the top of her hair. "No, Goldilocks. I don't think we are. Not today."

But one day we would. After all, I made her a promise.

The End.

———

THANK you for reading Out of the Gate! If you enjoyed Ada and Dermot you are going to love reading about how their grandchildren meet their matches in Off to the Races and A Photo Finish. Check them out on Amazon now! https://www.amazon.com/author/elsiesilver

Join my newsletter for exclusive content.

Keep reading for a sneak peek of each book!

OFF TO THE RACES EXCERPT

This.

This is my happy place.

No drama. No faking it. Just me and horses.

No human as far as the eye can see. Just the way I like it.

Anywhere with horses has always been my sanctuary, and this property is no exception. It's *immaculate*. Idyllic white fences outline the perfect green grass stretching out before me. And within each wooden square, a home to a beautiful shiny horse.

All layered with that comforting horse farm aroma I love.

I close my eyes and take a deep breath. No matter how pristine a farm is, you can't escape it, even outdoors. You can spend all the money in the world to keep your over-the-top, swanky facility spotless, and it will still smell like horse shit.

Makes me smile every time. Horses—1, humans—0.

I'm reveling in that score when a door slams behind me. I jump and turn around, hoping it's Hank, coming to wrap me in the best bear hug in the world. I peer through the fountain, centered in the driveway, expecting Hank's familiar frame, but it's not him. I'm met with an absolute vision far better in person than any of the pictures I found online.

Tall? Check.

Dark? Check.

Handsome? Check.

Looks like he wants to kill me? Also, check.

I run my teeth over my bottom lip as his tall, lithe body, wearing the hell out of a dark fitted suit, stalks toward me. Dark chocolate hair, longer on the top and a little disheveled—like he's been running his fingers through it, frames his annoyed face. Stubble blooms below razor sharp cheekbones as he stops in front of me and peers down a straight nose almost too masculine for the shapely, frowning lips beneath it.

Good thing I'm not one to cower because, at what has to be at least six foot three, this man is imposing.

Fiery mahogany eyes bore down on me. "You need to turn your sweet ass around, get in your car, and leave. Now."

Wow, what a greeting.

I tilt my head and search his face for some trace of humor. Finding none, I bark out a laugh. Because who talks to a person they've just met this way?

Okay, it was really more of a loud snort, but snort

laughs make normal people laugh. Right? I even giggle a little at myself, and think, "Hey, maybe he'll join in!" But no, not this fire-breathing dragon. He crosses his arms over a broad chest and continues to glare at me like I'm dirt beneath his expensive shoes. *Typical.*

"Pretty and slow to follow directions. Seems on par with every girl she's been serving up to me on a platter lately. This whole natural look is a fresh angle," he says, waving one arm up and down me like I'm a broodmare, "so, I'll give her that. Do pass my kudos on in that regard when you report back to my mother about your failed attempt to lock me down into some breathtakingly boring arranged relationship. I'd rather date a blow-up doll."

I rear back slightly at that last bit. Date a blow-up doll? Oof. Did he really just say that? The man practically handed me an alley-oop. I could make so many jokes here, but remind myself to keep it professional. Steeling myself, I take a deep breath, because this is about to get awkward. He clearly does not know who I am, but I've done a bit of homework, and know exactly who he is.

Vaughn Harding.

I've missed Hank like crazy. When I showed up on his doorstep looking for a job ten years ago, he took me in and gave me a lot more than employment. Work, advice, a place to live, even a good talking to when I needed it. He was the father figure always dreamed of. So when I heard working beside him on the west coast of Canada, I couldn't get on a plane fast enough. I mean, my working Visa was up so I had to leave my training position in Ireland, anyway. At least I knew where I was going and the name of the farm so I could do some research.

My internet stalking skills are so next level I almost added them as a bullet point to the skills section of my resume. In putting those skills to good use, I found two types of photos of this man populating the internet. Half of the images were Professional Vaughn, looking suave and serious in relation to his family's business ventures. The others were of Party Vaughn, looking charming and polished, usually at some glitzy event with a beautiful woman beaming on his arm.

Never the same woman from what I could find. And trust me, I *looked*.

An animalistic growl pulls me from my thoughts. "I said leave."

Is this fucking guy for real? As a general rule, my brain-to-mouth filter is a little relaxed. I've been an agitator since childhood and am well-versed in navigating situations where someone is ticked off. But this? This is new. Which is probably why I'm standing here silent and dumbfounded, staring like an idiot?

Before I can say something polite to diffuse the situation, he holds his arms out and widens those molten eyes at me as if to say, "Hello? What the fuck are you doing?"

And then... He. Stomps. His. Foot.

Like a toddler.

A soft giggle bubbles up out of my chest. I don't even try to hold it in. I am well acquainted with men like Vaughn Harding. Few truly dependable things in the world exist, but trust fund babies being douchebags is one you can count on.

Holding one hand up to stop him, I launch in, "Okay, first of all, I am downright fascinated by your blow-up doll preference. Can we table that for now but revisit it someday?" A sneer touches his lips. Ha. Didn't like that one. "Second, I'm a grown-ass woman, don't call me a girl. And third, when you're finished having this epic man-child meltdown," I wave my hand up and down his body like he did to me, "can you please let Hank know that Billie Black is here for her job interview?"

And then I beam at him with a big old cheesy smile.

In his defense, he visibly pales while smoothing his suit jacket down and standing straighter.

He repeats back to me, "Billie Black?"

"That's me."

"I...," He shakes his head. "But, you're not a man?"

"An astute observation, Mr. Harding," I reply with a smirk.

This is familiar territory for me. My name frequently confuses people; it doesn't bother me. It's a nickname and I could go by something else if I wanted, but I kind of enjoy people's confusion over my name. And this encounter is no exception.

"Hey, Billie girl!" a familiar deep voice calls from over my shoulder. "You made it!"

Hank Brandt. Man, just hearing that voice makes me smile. I turn immediately, leaving Vaughn there gaping, to take in the face of the warmest, gentlest man I know. Broad shoulders, close-cut sandy hair, and a ruddy, deeply lined face, a face that's spent decades working out in the sun, rush toward me.

I've missed him. Sometimes you're born into a family, and other times you choose them. And when you choose them, you know in your bones that they're right for you. And that's Hank for me. The family I've chosen.

Almost jogging, Hank goes right in for a big old bear hug. And I soak it up. "You're even more beautiful than the last time I saw you," he says, holding me back by my shoulders and taking me in.

I go pink in the cheeks and roll my eyes at him. "Stop sucking up, old man. You already got me here. Now, show me around."

Hank has been a pillar of support in both my childhood and in my professional career; a friend, a father-figure, and hopefully now an employer.

Assuming I haven't completely blown it with money-bags back there. Anxiety flutters in my stomach. I have my work cut out for me and will have to rise above that awkward introduction if I really want this job.

"Never lose that spunk, kiddo," he says, shaking his head and slinging an arm over my shoulder.

Hank leads me back towards Mr. Handsome-and-Crazy, who appears to have regained some composure.

"Billie, meet Vaughn Harding, the new owner and operator here at Gold Rush Ranch. He's a busy man, between this farm and the family mining business, but he'll be around for the foreseeable future managing our business operations." Vaughn stares down at me now with an unreadable expression. "He's going to sit in on the interview today to provide a second opinion. Hope that's okay with you."

I feel my throat bob as I swallow. That's great. Just great.

Stepping out from under Hank's arm, I extend my hand forward into Vaughn's strong grasp. I search for any signs of embarrassment on his part and find none. His face is stony and locked down now, all traces of the fiery passion he spit mere moments ago have completely disappeared.

Naturally, I test the waters by tossing him a quick wink while reciprocating his firm handshake. And by handshake, I mean death grip. I squeeze the hell out of his hand right back. Years of handling and riding powerful horses means I'm stronger than I look.

I think I might even hear him grunt under his breath when I clamp down around his fingers. "The more the merrier," I say. "It's a pleasure to meet you, Mr. Harding."

He nods as he drops my hand abruptly and then switches his focus on a spot over my head. "I'll be in my office when you're ready," he says to Hank before spinning on his heel and walking away, head held high, like he didn't just embarrass himself.

When I glance back at Hank, I see a twinkle in his eye as a slow Cheshire grin spreads across his face. Tutting me and shaking his head, he says, "Billie, Billie, Billie. What did you do to that poor boy?"

At that, I throw my head back and laugh. Poor boy? I'm well acquainted with men like Vaughn Harding. I grew up immersed in that culture. Rich and spoiled men like him never outgrow their arrogant entitlement. Instead, they wear it like some sort of badge of honor.

My Dad is exhibit A in that kind of behavior, followed by all the boys at boarding school and the men who mingled in our circles. Carbon copies of each other, the lot. Polished, calculated, and unfeeling.

Not to mention, boring.

And fake, fake, fake.

Fake smiles, fake friendships, fake family. And that last one is the real kicker. I felt my pretty, perfectly curated life crash down around me that day.

Surprisingly, being a shitty, misguided person isn't enough to make a little girl stop loving her dad. But it is enough to make me lose respect for him. And that is a heart-wrenching combination... loving someone you can't respect.

Even a decade later, years into adulthood, it hurts in a way that has the power to take my breath away.

My father's word might mean nothing anymore, but mine is still good. I kept the promise I made to myself—leave and never darken the door of that lifestyle again.

I went out in a real blaze of glory, and I've been in rebuilding mode ever since. My sole focus has been my career, and this opportunity is the perfect next step.

As I watch Vaughn, the embodiment of everything I ran away from, enter the building, I admire the physique within his tailored suit pants. Trim waist. Incredible ass. Ten out of ten would grab.

But I won't. Because I know this type of man. An absolute nightmare to interact with, dangerous to get involved with. But still fun to ogle. I am only human after all, and the man is hot as sin.

Yes, I will enjoy the hell out of this view, but from a safe distance. Because men like Vaughn are a trap I will never fall into.

Read Off to the Races now

A PHOTO FINISH EXCERPT

My mental checklist is overflowing as I pack the last of what I'll need into my little Volkswagen Golf. The one with rust patches above the wheel well and the chewed corner of the seat from when my favorite ranch dog was a puppy. The one I packed up and drove away from my family home when I finally set out on my own a little over two years ago. Some people might see a car that belongs in a junk pile. Me? I see my golden chariot to independence. I love this little car and everything it represents.

I stand back to assess everything I've stuffed into the back seat and blow a loose piece of hair off my face. It's the first big race day of the season, and I'm trying, poorly, to keep my nerves at bay. This season is my shot, my chance to prove myself as a real jockey. To prove that my Northern Crown wins last year weren't just a stroke of freshman luck. This job is supposed to be fun. Hard work, but fun. But today it just feels overwhelmingly heavy. The pressure weighs on me like an invisible lead vest. Even getting air into my lungs feels like it takes concentration.

I force myself to take a mental inventory of what's all here and shake my head when I realize what I've forgotten. "Shit. Right. My silks."

How great would that have been? Showing up to the track in Vancouver—which is at least an hour and a half from the farm here in Ruby Creek—without my Gold Rush Ranch silks. The black and gold uniform I wear every single race.

Shaking my head as I march back into the barn, I head down the long hall of offices toward the laundry room at the end. I live in a small apartment above the barn so I just do my laundry down here. I grew up on a proper ranch, in the dirt and snow, usually with hay in my hair, so the thought of washing all my clothes in the same machines used for the hairy horse laundry doesn't bother me at all.

I'm almost to the door when I hear it.

"Violet."

That voice. The low rumble of it. The threat woven into it. The man behind it. I swear my feet grow roots that shoot out and bind me to the ground. My heart knocks violently in my chest like it's trying to get out and run away. And quite frankly, I don't blame it. I want to get out of here too.

He wasn't supposed to be here yet. I was supposed to be gone down the highway by the time he showed up. He was supposed to be out of my life. I was supposed to have left him behind. Forgotten him.

But I haven't. I've warred with myself, wrestled and fought. Been with other men to prove to myself that I'm fine. But one word out of his mouth, and I seriously wonder if I am. I could run and hide, but that's not how the new me handles this. *The new Violet isn't a shrinking Violet.* That's what I keep telling myself anyway.

Maybe one day it will feel true.

So I suck in as much oxygen as I can and hold my head up high. I refuse to let this man make me feel small or embarrassed. We have a shared past, but we're both adults. *This will be fine.*

Spinning on one heel, I turn and march back to the office I just passed. The one that has sat empty for years. I stop just inside the doorway, partly because I don't want to go any further and partly because I'm reeling. All it takes is one look at Cole Harding, sitting behind a desk in a dark suit, spinning the cufflinks on his shirt, for me to lose all the bravado I just puffed myself up with. I literally feel it roll right off me like someone has doused me with a bucket of cold water. My body's reaction to him has never been normal, and today is no exception.

The inky hair, the gray eyes, the square shoulders, the sad tilt to his mouth. He crosses his arms under my gaze, and I roll my lips together at the sight. Just the way he moves, so sure and so calculated, drives me to distraction. There's so much power coiled in every inch of his body. A soldier's body.

His biceps are where my eyes land, and where they stay. They're incredible. I wonder how they'd look completely bare, how they'd feel wrapped around me. I hate myself for even going there. But I keep my eyes trained on them, because it's less unnerving than looking him in those soulful eyes. Silvery pools, deep and haunted and swirling with so much. The ones full of anger, and pain, and sorrow. Those are a much bigger problem for me. And for my heart.

"Violet." He says my name like it's a sentence, a full thought. Like I should know exactly what he means when he says it. But I don't know *anything* where Cole Harding is concerned. I think I actually know less than anything. Other than the hair on my arms is standing up like there's an electrical current running over me, and my stomach is flipping like I just shot down off the high point of a roller coaster. Which is apt, because my history with Cole is nothing if not a roller coaster.

"Everyone calls me Vi." I hate how quiet my voice comes out. I hate the way my name sounds on his lips, too formal and too familiar all at once.

His eyes rove my body, but he doesn't smile. It's not appreciative. It's more like he's assessing me, like I'm a mess that needs cleaning up and he's trying to figure out how. Shame lurches in my gut, flashes of the way he talked to me once and how it warmed me to my bones pop up in my head, but I do my best to will it away. I've worked too hard at moving on to go down that rabbit hole again.

"I'm not everyone," he says plainly.

I hiss as I suck air in, trying not to sound like I'm gasping for it. Trying not to give away the fact that he's just winded me with his words. Blood rushes in my ears and pools in my cheeks—like it always does. *You look so fucking pretty in pink.* He'd told me that once, and now it takes every ounce of my strength not to let my mind and body wander back to that day.

"What do you want, Cole?"

His eyes flash, and his body goes rigid right as his jaw ticks. Like somehow I'm the one who's annoying him when he's the one who called me in here. He could have kept his mouth shut, and I'd have been none the wiser. We could have avoided this entire encounter.

"I just want to make sure that we're on the same page. That we can continue to stay out of each other's way while I work out here. That you can keep things . . ." his eyes slide down my body and then back up, "professional."

Professional. Nothing between us has ever been professional. He's seen me naked, trampled my heart, and then showed back up out of nowhere with nothing but cool looks and mocking words and now expects *me* to keep things *professional*? Indignation flares up in me over the fact that he feels entitled to dictate how I should conduct myself. Like I don't come up against enough of that in this industry as it is. It's a sore spot, and he should know. I spent long nights telling him about my childhood. About how I struck out on my own. And now he's going to waltz in here and talk to me like *that*? No way.

"Let me be clear, Cole." This time I don't let my voice waver, and I don't stare at his biceps. I stare right into his steely eyes. "This is *my* place of work, and I am nothing if not professional. The way you're talking to *me* right now? It isn't professional. So, I'm going to continue doing exactly what I have been for the past year and *you* can stay out of *my* way. Think you can manage?"

His body snaps back slightly, and his eyes go wide. Like he didn't see that coming. Didn't see *me* coming. And he lashes out at me for it. I see the flash of insecurity on his face right before he spews his words back at me. And it's that hint of sorrow that takes the bite out of them.

"Pretty in Purple was so sweet. What happened?"

I shake my head at him sadly. Because when it comes down to it, that's what I feel when I see him, when I think of him. Sad.

"Seems like you mistook Pretty in Purple for a doormat."

I look at him just long enough to see the forlorn look on his face, the crack in his cold exterior, before I turn and walk away. The spear to my damn heart. Golddigger85 is just as lost as he was before, just as complicated. Just as broken. And I've already decided I won't tolerate the way he lashes out. *We all make choices.* That's what he told me once, and he wasn't wrong.

It's why I moved on. It's why I disappeared without a word. It's why this awkwardness between us now is on him, not me. My head knows exactly what choices to make where Cole Harding is concerned.

But my heart?

It's not so sure.

Read A Photo Finish now

BOOKS BY ELSIE SILVER

The Gold Rush Ranch Series

Out of the Gate

Off to the Races

A Photo Finish

The Front Runner

AFTERWORD

Thank you for reading Out of the Gate! I hope you enjoyed Ada and Dermot's story as much as I enjoyed writing it.

If you want to stay in the loop with upcoming releases, or be first in line for future exclusive scenes and giveaways, join The Silver Society mailing list. Or even just swing by and say hi on social media. I would love to hear from you!

Finally, a review on Amazon or Goodreads would mean the world to me. It only takes a few moments and makes such a big difference for an indie author.

ACKNOWLEDGMENTS

This story is short and sweet, but boy were there a lot of people behind the scenes helping me get this together (holding my hand). Melanie Harlow, without you this book would have had a mafia romance cover and a paranormal romance blurb. How freaking lucky am I to have someone like you in my corner? I seriously pinch myself. Casey, your eye for design and unflappable patience with my non-stop questions is admirable. You're the real MVP. And Kylie, thank you for your time and seriously detailed feedback—this story would be very different without your keen eye. It's a special skill! I'm telling you.

Finally, a big thank you to my husband, for keeping me sane and being the best cheerleader a girl could ask for. You look cute in that skirt, babe. And to my son, for helping me choose the cover photo. ("Who is dad kissing in this picture?")

ELSIE SILVER

Elsie Silver is a Canadian author of sassy, sexy, small town romance who loves a good book boyfriend and the strong heroines who bring them to their knees. She lives just outside of Vancouver, British Columbia with her husband, son, and three dogs and has been voraciously reading romance books since before she was probably supposed to.

She loves cooking and trying new foods, traveling, and spending time with her boys—especially outdoors. Elsie has also become a big fan of her quiet five o'clock mornings, which is when most of her writing happens. It's during this time that she can sip a cup of hot coffee and dream up a fictional world full of romantic stories to share with her readers.

www.elsiesilver.com

Made in the USA
Middletown, DE
13 October 2023